A
Brown Bird
Singing

FRANCES WOSMEK

ILLUSTRATIONS BY TED LEWIN

Lothrop, Lee & Shepard Books

New York

1 2 3 4 5 6 7 8 9 10

Library of Congress Cataloging-in-Publication Data
Wosmek, Frances.   A brown bird singing.
Summary: Left by her father to be raised by his white friends in a small Minnesota town, a Chippewa
Indian girl is afraid he will return and take her away from the only family she remembers.
[1. Chippewa Indians—Fiction.   2. Indians of North America—Fiction.   3. Family life—
Fiction.   4. Minnesota—Fiction] I. Title.
PZ7.W884Br 1986   [Fic]   85-24002
ISBN 0-688-06251-2

A
Brown Bird
Singing

DEDICATED TO THE MEMORY
OF MY PARENTS

A
Brown Bird
Singing

CHAPTER ONE

The Last Day
of School

❧ ❧   Anego was the only Indian in the school. She might just as well have been the only Indian anywhere. Almost everyone she knew had pale skin, hair like ripe wheat, and eyes the color of the sky.

It was quite a long time ago. The small white schoolhouse stood in a cold northern corner of Minnesota. The school was almost hidden by thick green pine trees. On most maps not even a tiny dot marked the tight little mostly Scandinavian community that spread out over the low hills, small farms, and lakes surrounding the schoolhouse.

This day Anego sat as tall as anyone at her seat in the fourth-grade row. Because it was the last day of school, she was wearing her best white eyelet dress with a blue ribbon sash and long white stockings. The ends of her sleek black braids were tied with crisp blue ribbons.

More than anything Anego was proud of her brand-new boots from the Sears Roebuck catalog. There was a pocket on the side of one of them. In it was a shiny new jackknife.

"Those are boys' boots," her sister, Sheila, had scoffed as Mama wrote out the order.

"I know," Anego had replied, "but the knife is free."

Today the schoolroom was a happy place. Anego's damp fingers folded and unfolded the sheet of paper with the piece she was to say. From time to time she gathered courage to peek back over her shoulder. With each new arrival her heart pounded even harder. Her throat felt tight and dry. Her ears throbbed. Speaking in front of so many people was more than she could clearly imagine herself doing. She felt trapped and terrified, but at the same time she trembled with a strange, wild kind of excitement.

She glanced across the room at Pa. His folding chair was tipped back, balanced on two legs, leaning against the blackboard. For one brief moment Angeo held his cool gaze. You can do it. There is nothing in the world to be afraid of, his blue eyes plainly said.

Anego had lived with Mama and Pa and Sheila for a long time. She was a Chippewa Indian. She had always known that. Someday, when Hamigeesek, her real father, returned, she would go back to her own people. She had heard the story more times than she could count. Her mother had died of the fever when Anego was very small. Many others in the Indian community had died as well. Hamigeesek, needing to move on with the rest to hunt and gather the wild rice, had left Anego with his white friend. There he knew she would be well, safe, and happy until he could return for her.

"He was my good friend," Pa was always careful to add. "He loved you so much he chose the safest place for you that he knew, even though it meant leaving you behind. Things may not have gone as he had planned. But someday he will be back. You will see."

But the years slipped by, and he had not returned.

In the dim corners of her memory, Anego could remember having been very frightened and lonely. When she had closed her eyes at night, she heard the coyotes yelp and bark at the full moon rising over Pa's hill. Then she had remembered her mother's face smiling down at her. It told her to be brave and not to be afraid.

As time passed, her mother's face and the music of

3

her words had faded. Nothing was left but a feeling that was soft, warm, and trembling to escape. It was like a brown bird she had once held in her hands. The bird had flown away, but she had always remembered it. Even now, just thinking about the bird brought back the soft, warm feeling. It reminded her to be brave and not to be afraid.

Suddenly the schoolroom was filled with a burst of good-natured clapping. The conversation and scattered laughter died away. All attention was directed toward the front of the room.

Miss Anderson waited for the clapping to stop. She twirled the new ring on her finger. Miss Anderson was leaving to be married. There would be a new teacher next year.

"Mothers and fathers, boys and girls," Miss Anderson began, forming her words exactly.

Miss Anderson's brown hair was marcelled in tight, even waves. She wore a white middy blouse with a sailor collar and long black tie. Her skirt was blue with pleats. She looked just like the pictures in Mama's magazines, Anego thought, beaming with pride and admiration.

"The children and I are pleased to have all of you as our guests on this last day of school," Miss Anderson went on. She glanced at her notes as she spoke. "The first number on our program will be a song sung by Mrs. Veselka, who has brought her harp and has kindly agreed to entertain us."

Anego squirmed in her seat. She flushed with pleasure at the applause that followed Mama to the front of the room. Mama took her small harp from its case and sat on the folding chair placed center stage, in front of everyone.

Mama was from a faraway country called Ireland. She had naturally curly hair, as rich and red as autumn leaves. She sang and played the harp. Anego was very proud of Mama. Most of the other mothers, in Anego's eyes, were very ordinary. They were simple, practical people with Swedish accents who made fancy cakes for basket socials.

Mama did not make such fancy cakes. Her Irish cakes were always plain and flavored with lots of caraway seeds.

But none of the other mothers could measure up to Mama as she smilingly took her place, fingered the harp lightly, and sang her Irish songs. Everyone thought so, Anego knew.

When it came time for Anego to say her piece, Miss Anderson leaned across the aisle. "Now, remember,

Anego," she reminded softly, "speak loud and clear."

Anego, her hands as cold as ice, stared at a spot on the floor. She recited the words as fast as she could. As soon as she was through, she glanced quickly at Pa's face, ducked back into her seat, and dropped her eyes. She flushed at the sound of clapping from all sides. As always, it had turned out to be a lot easier than she had feared.

Sheila had a longer piece. Sheila would be in the eighth grade next year. For a long time Mama had been telling Pa that when Sheila graduated it would be time for them to move closer to a high school.

"It would be different if Sheila had been a boy," Mama would sometimes say. "More than likely a boy would want to take over the homestead someday."

"It's good land," Pa would reply with a sigh. "I have worked hard to clear it. I built a better house than any around."

"I know," Mama would agree. "But a good education can do no harm. The world is changing fast, Pa."

"Of course," Pa would always say. "We will do what is best for the girls."

Anego avoided Mama's eyes at times like that. She knew that Mama would be looking at her, her eyes full of worry and questioning. She knew that Mama would be thinking, What about Anego? What plans can we make for her? Someday, maybe tomorrow, Hamigeesek will return to take her away forever. He will want her to be with her own people again.

Then Anego would reach back in her memory, desperately searching for the brown bird. It always appeared in time to remind her that she must be brave and not afraid.

In Ireland Mama had lived with her parents and brothers and sisters in a city filled with people. She talked about her family often, remembering the green fields of the Irish countryside and the many friends she would never see again. Then, more than likely, she would sigh and softly say, "It's lovely here, but I do get so *hungry* to see more people."

Pa's parents had come by boat from the little country of Austria. They had traveled to Minnesota by wagon train. Pa had been born on their homestead. Years later, Pa got a homestead of his own. He cleared the land and built the house himself, with only the help of a few neighbors. It was the first house for miles around to have hardwood floors. Pa had painted it sunshine yellow. He was very proud of his house.

Miss Anderson closed the program with a short farewell speech and the passing out of report cards.

Anego slipped her card from its envelope beneath the desk top, away from prying eyes. She felt a mild glow of pleasure as she read the words "Promoted to the fifth grade." However, Miss Anderson's neat little scribble wound up into the card's margin. "Anego could do much better if only she were not so shy," it said.

Anego was not very interested in marks. That she had passed would please Mama. That she had passed by very little made no difference to Anego at all.

Everyone was shouting and waving cards in the air in gay, high spirits.

"I passed! I passed! Did you pass?"

On this last day, Miss Anderson did not seem to mind the noise.

The men, loud and jolly, gathered around the pump in the side yard. They pumped buckets of fresh, clear water for the horses that had been tied to trees behind the schoolhouse all morning.

Miss Anderson, together with the mothers and upper-grade girls, spread the picnic lunch on table-cloths on the grass. There were salads, sandwiches, and fancy cakes. There was homemade ice cream. There were paper plates for everyone.

Mama had brought sandwiches. Sheila had been careful to offer Mama's sandwiches. It would be a mistake, she knew, to let Mama bring one of her caraway cakes.

"Your mother doesn't know how to make cakes!" Eric Swanson, who was in her class, had once told Sheila.

"She could if she wanted to, smarty-pants!" Sheila had replied. Sheila was big for her age. She stood up to everyone, boys included.

Sheila had sounded so fierce that Eric had backed off in a hurry. He made sure there was a safe distance between them. Then he shouted back over his shoulder, "Sheila's mother's cakes are bread! Sheila's mother's cakes are bread!"

The picnic spread was more food than Anego had ever seen at one time. She forgot all about her usual fussy appetite. She heaped her paper plate with every good thing it would hold.

"Don't be greedy, Anego," Mama warned from the opposite end of the tablecloth. "If you take too much, you know you will only waste it." But Mama's face was smiling, caught up in the spirit of the day.

Anego smiled back. Then she followed Mildred Algren, her best friend, to look for a place in the shade. She gripped her plate firmly with both hands.

Mildred's pale blue eyes studied Anego's new boots with interest. "Those are boys' boots," she noted.

"I know," Anego said with a nod, "but the knife was free."

Mildred and her brothers were the only children who lived close enough to school to go home for lunch. Mildred always knew the teacher better than anyone because her family "boarded" the teacher. Mildred would often invite Anego to walk home with her at lunchtime. Anego would unpack her lunchbox on the sewing machine and eat her lunch without a word. Mrs. Algren, with Mildred and her five tow-headed brothers, filled all the space around their small table. Anego would watch and listen, feeling glad she had just Sheila and not five noisy brothers.

Mildred passed by a number of shady spots before she found one that seemed exactly right.

"You sit over there," she said, spreading her own lunch in the thickest shade.

Anego could see that the shade Mildred offered was laced with ribbons of hot sun. It was probably enough to melt the ice cream. But she took the place pointed out to her. She moved her plate with the ice cream as the shade moved.

"Your ma is pretty," Mildred said. "You sure don't look like her."

"I know," Anego said. She was glad that Mildred

thought Mama was pretty. Mildred was usually right about everything.

"I suppose that's because she ain't your real ma," Mildred went on. "I suppose, being an Indian, your real ma looked like a squaw."

Anego filled her mouth with potato salad and did not reply.

There were games and prizes in the afternoon. Following Mildred's lead, Anego entered them all. She did not expect to win anything. The big race at the end was a free-for-all. Everyone was invited, it was announced.

"The winner," Miss Anderson said with awe in her voice, "will be awarded a brand-new, shiny silver dollar!"

A soft, breathless murmur swept through the crowd of children and parents who had huddled in anxious, good-natured groups to watch.

A whole silver dollar! Anego had never owned so much money. But as she glanced down the line her hopes dwindled. She could see Mildred's determined face. She could see Sheila crouched into starting position. Every single upper-grader was there.

She took the time to glance over her shoulder at Pa. He smiled and winked an encouraging wink. Anego smiled back.

"Go!"

Almost before the word was out of Miss Anderson's mouth, the line was off and running.

Anego gritted her teeth and ran as fast as she could. Just the same, she could see that the others were passing her fast.

Then "Take it easy. Keep it steady. Don't tire yourself out at the beginning. Keep enough energy for a strong finish." She could almost hear Pa's cool, calm voice urging her on through deep snow or when she was rowing a boat across the lake.

She drew a long, deep breath. She felt her muscles relax. She pretended she was a deer racing through the meadow, tucking its neat hoofs in, flying over the cowslips, and sailing over the fences. Anego felt alive and free and full of happiness.

Everyone seemed surprised when she crossed the finish line first. But Anego was not surprised. Whoever heard of anyone running faster than a deer?

The silver dollar felt smooth and cool in her hot hand. She ducked through the crowd, looking for Mildred. With a happy smile she reached out and uncurled her fingers.

"Look!" she said. "I won the dollar!"

Mildred's light skin was red with sunburn. Her gay,

starched dress was limp. Her pale, rag-wound curls had lost their bounce.

"It wasn't fair," she said. "My ma said it wasn't a fair race. You are an Indian. Indians are used to running."

The smile faded from Anego's face. She could feel her cheeks burn. She slipped the dollar into her pocket and turned away without another word.

The mothers gathered the children together and cleared the remains of the picnic. The men went off to untie the horses and lead them around to their waiting families.

Dick and Daisy pawed the ground gently and neighed softly when they saw Pa. He took the time to scratch their foreheads. They nuzzled their soft noses against the front of his shirt in reply. Eager to be off, they pranced rather than walked as Pa led them around to the front.

He held their bridles firmly. Mama climbed into the front seat of the buggy. She tucked her harp gently in at the foot. Sheila and Anego scrambled in behind. They sat on soft hay that had been covered with a blanket.

Pa gave the reins a slap. Dick and Daisy sprinted into a lively trot. They wheeled the buggy out of the schoolyard in a cloud of dust.

"Well," said Mama, settling back with a laugh. "I guess Anego showed them!"

Pa smiled, looking pleased.

Anego fingered the cool silver dollar in her pocket. The warm feathers of the brown bird softly brushed her memory.

Sheila shifted her position to face Anego. "Did you pass?" she wanted to know.

Anego nodded.

"I don't believe it," Sheila said. "Show me your card."

Anego slid the card from its envelope and held it out proudly. "See! I told you I did!"

Sheila studied the card carefully. Then she turned it sideways and read, " 'Anego could do much better if only she were not so shy,' That means," she said with a little smile, "that you almost didn't pass."

Facing the back, Anego watched the road unroll behind them like a long, dusty ribbon. Spring rains had left puddles in the low places. The spinning buggy wheels wove two threads of narrow tracks dipping in and out of the puddles. Overgrown branches slapped the sides of the buggy. Anego held out her hand and let the branches brush by.

Pa stopped the horses in front of the gate.

In an instant, Anego gripped the edge of the buggy and dropped to the ground. She lifted the latch on the big old wooden gate and swung it to one side for Pa to drive through.

Goldie, Star, and Tuesday, the three brown cows, were standing ankle-deep in the tender spring clover. They slid their jaws from side to side and watched the homecoming with soft chocolate-brown eyes.

Gyp, the black dog, had been waiting on the front porch all day. He raced to meet them, yelping for joy. He thrashed his tail with wide, happy sweeps.

The yellow house was perched on the crest of a small green hill. It caught the rays of the setting sun, turning the windows to gold. The house looked comfortable and peaceful. Its pillared porch reached around two sides. Sheila and Anego often roller-skated there on rainy days.

The air was fragrant with the sweet smell of lilacs. The cooing and chirping of a family of martins could be heard coming from the birdhouse.

Pa's eyes scanned the scene like those of an anxious mother hen. Then, satisfied that all was in order, he sighed with contentment, as he always did when he returned home after having been away.

While Pa unharnessed the horses, Mama set about

making the supper. She lit the kindling in the range. She filled the big old coffee pot with fresh water from the pump outside the kitchen door.

"Sheila," she said, handing her a bowl of boiled potatoes from the day before, "do slice these up for frying. Anego, run on down to the cellar and bring up something canned that won't take too long."

It took Anego a long time to find what she wanted. The cellar was cool and dark. Anego imagined things in the dark. She saw moving shapes and felt the presence of things she could not quite see. The cellar smelled musty. She brushed against cobwebs. She closed her eyes, feeling the way and trying not to think.

Hugging a cold glass jar of string beans against her warm front, Anego began her climb back up the steps. She could see the friendly beam of light from the kitchen. She could hear the sizzle of potatoes frying in Mama's pan. She heard footsteps above, and the low, steady hum of Mama's and Pa's voices.

Then suddenly Mama's voice rose sharply. "You heard from Hamigeesek?" she cried. "Why didn't you tell me?"

Anego stopped abruptly. Cold prickles shivered up her spine. She could feel her heart pounding like a warrior's tom-tom against the cool glass jar of string beans.

"There was no need to worry you," Pa was saying. "It was only hearsay. It might never amount to a thing."

"What might never amount to a thing?" Mama cried.

"Well," Pa began in his slow way, "seems this old trapper stopped by the post office last week. Turned out he knew Hamigeesek real well. It appears this feller did some asking around about us. He wanted to know if we were still on the homestead, and if we still had Anego with us."

There was a pause. Anyone could have heard a feather fall. Anego hardly dared breathe.

Pa hesitated as though he would rather not go on. Anego strained forward to hear.

"He said that Hamigeesek himself might be back before too long."

Anego moved up the last steps slowly on numb feet. She walked across the kitchen and placed the jar of beans carefully on the table.

"Mercy, child!" Mama exclaimed, whirling around and looking startled. "I didn't hear you come up." Then she added briskly, without looking, "Now, run

17

on out and get some fresh air while Sheila and I set the table."

Anego could see that only her mouth was smiling. Her eyes were brimming over with tears.

Gyp, sunning himself in the warm straw by the barnyard door, pricked his ears. Then he raced to meet Anego, wagging his tail, inviting a game.

But Anego paid no attention at all. Her thoughts were far away. She shivered in the warm sunshine. And not even the brown bird could do a thing about the feeling of fear and helplessness that had come to sweep away all the joy of the day.

CHAPTER TWO

Pa's Kind
of Surprise

When Anego awoke on the first morning of summer vacation, she lay in bed, stretching her toes to their very limit under the covers. She thought of the whole day ahead. It was good to know that it belonged to her, that she was free to use it in any way she chose.

She heard Pa's quiet tread on the stairs, moving step by step to the bottom. She heard him open the outside door and close it softly behind him. Pa always checked his animals first thing each morning.

Anego rolled over. She watched a small wink of sunlight dance on the windowsill from a tiny hole no bigger than a pinprick in the dark green shade.

In almost no time, she could feel her first pleasant

thoughts slipping away. A dull remembering spread and swelled inside, squeezing into her breathing. Until yesterday Hamigeesek had been only a shadowy figure belonging to the past, like Mama's stories of Ireland, or Pa's growing up on a Minnesota homestead. He had been part of something that had happened a long, long time ago, something that could be tucked away and forgotten when the story was ended.

Now Hamigeesek had come alive. He was real. He was coming to take her away. He was going to make her into an Indian. Anego pulled the covers over her head. She curled into a tight ball. She felt lonely and afraid. I don't want to be an Indian, she thought. I want to live here. I want to be like Pa and Ma and Sheila.

She heard the downstairs door open and close after Pa as he came back inside.

"Anego!" His voice from the foot of the stairs was loud enough to be heard only by someone who was already awake. Pa knew for certain she would be.

"I have a surprise for you!"

Anego threw back the covers and sprang from her bed. Magically, all disturbing thoughts of Hamigeesek hurried out of the way, disappearing into the deep part of her mind where they belonged.

She knew the excitement of Pa's kind of surprises,

likely to be new kittens or even a new baby calf. These were the special secrets Pa and Anego shared long before Mama and Sheila were awake.

Groping in the half-light, she hurried into the clothes most handy. She bolted out the door and down the stairs, threading her arms through the sleeves of her jacket and fastening buttons on the way.

Pa was being very mysterious. "You'll see," was all he would reply to Anego's flood of eager questions.

Out in the cool morning air, the sun was just climbing into sight over the tops of the trees. Pa's and Anego's feet left a trail of printed tracks in the fresh dew.

Anego trotted to keep up with Pa's long stride as he made his way around behind the barn. He chose the trail that led to the meadow where Goldie, Star, and Tuesday spent their days growing fat on the fresh long grass.

A breeze stirred softly. It whispered overhead through the dense green branches of the pine and spruce trees. The clear flutelike notes of the redwing blackbirds rippled from the meadow. Now and then the bright, musical voice of the meadowlark announced to all who would listen, "Spring of the year! Spring of the year!"

Motioning Anego to be quiet, Pa slowed his pace.

He chose each step carefully, moving with hardly a sound. Then he stopped.

Anego, just as carefully, moved up to stand by his side. One glance, and she raised questioning eyes to Pa's face. Just a poor dead deer, she was thinking. What kind of a surprise is that?

"Look hard," Pa told her softly. "You won't see it unless you look very hard."

Anego looked again. The dead deer was easy enough to see. Pa could never have meant that. She moved her eyes slowly over the dry leaves and the new green curls of little ferns. She was careful to notice the purple mayflowers waving their heads, each perched on the top of a delicate, hairy stem. She could see patches of wintergreen shining in the moss. Then she caught her breath in surprise and delight.

There, among last year's leftover leaves and dry brown pine needles, lay a tiny velvet-eyed fawn. Not one muscle moved. Only if you looked very carefully could you be sure that it was breathing at all.

Pa was leaning over the mother deer. He moved its limbs. He turned its head from side to side. "She doesn't have any marks," he said. "She probably has been poisoned. She may have gotten into some bait put out for the wolves."

"But what about the baby?" Anego's voice was anx-

ious and excited. "Is it all right? Why doesn't it move?"

"A wild baby, even as young as this one, knows by instinct that it has a better chance to survive if it stays perfectly still where its mother has hidden it. See how nature has given it a coat that matches its surroundings exactly."

Pa squatted on his heels for a closer look. Anego squatted on hers beside him.

The early sunlight flickered and shimmered, blending the fawn's spotted coat with the dry leaves. Only the wide, frightened brown eyes looked alive and real.

Anego reached out and gently stroked the little animal's soft coat. With her fingertips she could feel it shiver. She could feel the rise and fall of its new breathing.

"Let's take it home, Pa," she pleaded.

Pa hesitated. "A wild animal needs an awful lot of care," he said. "A baby like this would have to be fed very often, day and night. Who would ever want to go to all that trouble just to keep a little fawn alive?"

Anego gave Pa a startled look. "Oh, Pa, I would! I would!" Then she laughed softly at the twinkle in Pa's eyes.

"Well," he said, "maybe you'll be sorry, but if we

don't take him, the wolves or coyotes will be sure to."

All the way home Anego kept a watchful eye on the little fawn, its long legs dangling from Pa's arms. As she hurried along behind, her thoughts slipped back to the uneasy feelings she had all but forgotten in the excitement. Pa was the very best friend she had ever had. Would he let her real father take her away? The more she thought about it, the more certain she was that he would not. Pa would never let her go.

Anego held the fawn while Pa folded a warm woolen blanket and put it into a cardboard box. He placed the box behind the kitchen range, and Anego gently laid the fawn inside.

"He will need a name," Pa reminded her, smiling.

Anego had named a great many kittens and calves, even baby chickens and pigs, but she had never had to name anything quite so splendid as a fawn before. Not just any ordinary name would do.

"How about an Indian name?" Pa suggested. "I once knew a Chippewa boy called Magwah. How about that?"

Anego did not look at Pa. She did not want an Indian name. She did not want an Indian anything. But she knew that Pa was only trying to please her, and so she nodded.

25

Things took a practical turn with Mama up and bustling about the kitchen. She filled the old coffee pot and stirred the lumps from the oatmeal.

"The little thing must be hungry," she said with a quick glance. "It should have a bottle. It can never drink from a pail like the calves. It's far too young."

Pa was already warming a little milk in a pan. He showed Sheila and Anego how to dip their fingers in the milk and hold them, dripping, beneath the fawn's nose, waiting for him to lick it off.

Just as Mama had said, Magwah was hungry. It took him no time at all to learn. He tickled his tongue across their wet fingers, wagging his stump of a tail.

"As soon as the store is open," Pa said, "you girls can run down and ask if they have a bottle. It will take a long time to fill up a hungry fawn this way."

It was a mile to the general store. Usually Sheila and Anego took their time. They might stop on the little bridge over the creek and dangle their bare feet for a while. They might comb their fingers through the cold water looking for the jellied masses of frogs' eggs. There were sun-ripened strawberries and raspberries to be sampled in season. There were chokecherries to pucker their mouths and blacken their tongues.

The dusty road wound between rail fences to the top of a long hill. This was a stretch that needed to be

26

passed by quickly and quietly. There must be no loud voices. A red bull lived on the other side of the rails with a lazy group of cud-chewing cows. If the bull saw them he would come galloping. Sometimes he would bellow and paw up the ground. Then Sheila and Anego, puffing up the long hill, would run for their lives.

Today there was no time for anything. Magwah was hungry. They hurried over the bridge with hardly a glance on either side. Luckily, the red bull was no-where to be seen. Just the same, their conversation stopped with the beginning of the rail fence.

The long, silent walk up the hill gave Anego time to think. Hamigeesek and all the fears that went with him crowded back into her mind.

They rounded the crest of the hill. With all danger past, Anego suddenly felt the need to share her fears. Kicking up the dust with some small skipping steps, she fell into line with Sheila.

Sheila had a way that Anego envied. Sheila's eyes were cool and blue. She decided quickly and firmly what she wanted. Then she moved in a straight line to-ward whatever it was. She seldom failed. At least that was the way it looked to Anego.

Anego could see that Sheila was thinking, and maybe not in the best mood for listening. She was humming a tune from one of Pa's Victrola records under her breath. She rattled the coins in her apron pocket with each step. Her yellow hair rippled over her shoulders, catching the sun like ripe grain in a summer breeze.

"I heard Pa say something last night," Anego began.

"Hmmmmmmm," Sheila paused in her humming long enough to murmur. Then she went right on humming.

"It was something about my real father," Anego said in a louder voice. She knew this was a subject that never failed to arouse curiosity from anyone, including Sheila.

She was right. Sheila stopped humming and looked interested.

"What about him?" she asked.

"He's coming." Anego cleared her throat quickly. It would never do to cry. Sheila often said that only babies cried.

"He is?" Sheila was, at once, all attention. "When?"

Anego shrugged. It was all that she could trust herself to do.

"Is he coming to take you away?" Sheila asked directly, but so kindly that new tears seemed about to drown all Anego's good efforts so far.

Anego nodded miserably.

"He can't do that!" declared Sheila angrily. "He can't give you away, and then come and take you back, just like that! I'll tell you what," she said in a comfortingly fierce way. "We won't let him. I'll ask Mama and Pa to send him away. Maybe you could hide. We could tell him you have gone away and we don't know where."

Anego nodded. Tears were streaking down her cheeks, but Sheila did not seem to mind that she was crying. The tears were partly from relief. She felt a lot better having Sheila know. Sheila would think of something. She always did.

Before they reached the general store, Anego wanted to be sure of one thing. "Don't tell Mama and Pa that I heard," she said.

"I won't," Sheila promised.

"Cross your heart?"

"Cross my heart."

Magwah took to the bottle like an old-timer. He balanced on his long, unsteady legs. His hollow sides swelled out, round and firm, in no time at all. His tail dipped and waved like a small Fourth of July flag.

Pa had been right. He did need a great many more meals than Anego would have dreamed. But, true to her word, she put the cardboard box beside her bed at night and kept a fresh bottle of milk in a handy spot nearby. Each time Magwah thumped and bumped against the sides of the box, Anego rolled sleepily out of bed. She gripped the bottle firmly and held on until he was satisfied.

"Lucky it is for that wee deer that he has the likes of Anego to look after him," Mama said, shaking her head.

Pa's hand rested briefly on Anego's sleek black hair. "Hamigeesek would be proud of her," he said quietly. "She has inherited his knack with wild things. I learned from him much of what I know about them."

Anego paid almost no attention at all. For the time being, at least, Hamigeesek seemed very far away. The fact was clear that Magwah needed her. She was just as certain that Pa did too.

CHAPTER THREE
Summertime

≫ ≫   As Mama said often throughout the summer, Magwah was certainly growing like a weed. He outgrew the cardboard box very soon and took free run of the house and barnyard.

At first he was never far from Anego's side. He followed her everywhere. He nudged his way into her games. He demanded her attention. But he rewarded her with love brimming from his soft brown eyes.

It had taken some time to teach Gyp that the small, frisky fawn had settled into his territory for good. Gyp's position of importance had never been challenged before. Now that it was, he did the only thing he could. He pretended not to notice.

It was not long before Magwah began to feel the

need for more adventure. His curiosity about the world outside the barnyard grew. Sometimes he would streak off and race through the woods by himself. He always returned, but when he did, his eyes were shining with a mysterious, wild gleam. He was beginning to find the world on the other side of the rail fences more interesting than the slow, lazy pace of the barnyard.

"He is a wild creature," Pa said. "He needs space and freedom just as much as he needs food. But there are hunters in the woods who take no notice of the game laws. When the hunting season opens in the fall, it will be even more dangerous. When buck fever strikes, those city fellers will shoot anything that moves."

"Magwah can run very fast," Anego replied hopefully.

Pa shook his head. "By taming him we have taken away his fear of man, which is a deer's natural protection. Magwah would be easy prey for a hunter. He thinks of all people as his friends."

So Pa hung a jingling bell on a collar around Magwah's neck. "That's about all we can do," he said. "At least any hunter who will take the trouble to look can see that he is someone's pet."

Magwah was learning to glide through the bushes

with hardly a sound. He was not too pleased with a jingle that followed him everywhere.

"It's for your own good," Anego explained over and over. "It's for sure that a little bell is a whole lot better than getting shot."

In the full heat of the summer everything slowed. Pa unhitched Dick and Daisy when the noontime sun shone hot. The horses drank from a tub filled with cool water. Then, switching at flies with their long brown tails, they rolled in the dust.

Pa mopped his forehead. He sipped tall, cool glasses of lemonade before going back to the fields.

For Anego summer was a time of adventure and magic. She waded in the cold water of the frog pond, gathering long-stemmed water lilies. She discovered nests filled with eggs. They hatched into naked, wobbly little birds with wagging beaks. She watched the soft down turn into feathers. She held her breath while the young birds clung to the edges of their nests, gathering courage to spread their wings and fly.

As the summer wore on, Sheila's light skin took on a smooth, even tan. It deepened to a shade that nearly matched Anego's. But Sheila's sun-bleached yellow hair was a sharp contrast to Anego's braids, sleek and black as a crow's wing.

From the first day of vacation Sheila, as outgoing as Mama, had combed the countryside looking for friends. Sun-baked, shriveled little ladies and lonely old gentlemen were all warm-heartedly counted among her summer friends.

But the fact that half the summer had gone by, and Anego had not spent a minute of it wishing for the company of anyone, seemed unnatural to Mama.

"Why don't I ring up Mildred's mother?" she finally suggested. "Perhaps Mildred can come and spend a day with you."

Anego thought for a moment before she replied. Mildred belonged in school. She had never thought of her as being any other place. "Why?" she asked.

"Because you need friends," Mama said with a sigh. "Everyone needs friends."

"I have Magwah," Anego reminded her, "and Gyp."

But Mama had already made up her mind. She eyed the new telephone on the wall. It stared back at her with its two round bell-eyes. She cranked the small handle on the side: two short, two long, and then two more short rings. She spoke directly and clearly into the mouthpiece. She carefully held the receiver away from her ear.

Anego thrilled at the sound of Mama's loud, precisely spoken "Hello, Mrs. Algren." Being able to speak to someone three miles away was a miracle almost too great to believe.

Mildred was unloaded at the front door a few mornings later by her red-faced, red-haired father. He had a full day's work ahead of him, and so he trotted the horses and buggy briskly down the driveway and out of sight almost immediately.

Mildred looked strange, not at all as she did at school. Her face was covered with new freckles from the sun. She was wearing a dress Anego had never seen, very new and with hardly a crease. She had a new haircut too. Every straight, pale hair was cut to the same length, exactly to the tips of her earlobes.

Things started off badly. Sheila had gone off to visit one of her new friends. Even though Anego knew Mildred better than anyone at school, she felt shy. She had no idea what she was expected to do with her.

Magwah came to the rescue. He nuzzled Mildred's knees. He nibbled her hand. No one, not even Mildred, could resist the friendliness shining in his eyes. Anego forgot her shyness long enough to tell his story. But when Magwah wandered off, the conversation wandered off with him.

Gyp did his best to help. He wagged his tail cheerfully. He brought Mildred a stick to throw.

Mildred dusted a patch on the porch steps with her

hand and sat on it. She smoothed the skirt of her new dress across her thin knees. She eyed Gyp with mild interest. "My father says that Indians eat dogs," she said. "Do they?"

Anego's eyes widened with horror. "Of course not!" she declared. "Nobody eats dogs."

"Indians do," Mildred said. "My father says so."

For a minute Anego felt as dizzy as she sometimes did when she was swinging too high. She looked at Gyp. He was shoving the stick closer to Mildred's feet with his black nose.

"When your Indian father comes to take you away," Mildred went on to say, "you had better not let him see Gyp. He might get eaten."

Even in the warm sun, Anego felt chilled from head to toe. She did not actually believe Mildred. But all the old doubts and fears were back, together with another she could never even have imagined. She glanced down the driveway, hoping to see Mildred's father coming to take her home. But there was no sign of him.

It was not until after lunch, when Mama served big chunks of her caraway cake, that the day finally took off.

"I saw the teacher we're getting next year," Mildred announced suddenly.

Anego sat straight in her chair. She laid down her fork. She looked interested. Mildred always knew more about the teachers than anyone else.

"You did?"

Mildred nodded. Her pale, limp, newly cut hair slipped forward, hiding her freckled face. "She came to our house last night to see my father."

On top of everything else, Mildred's father was a member of the school board.

"She's fat, and she talks a lot."

"Is she nice?" Anego hurried to lead her on.

"Kind of."

"What do you mean . . . kind of?"

"Well, she would be nice, if it weren't for . . . "

"Weren't for what?" Anego moved to the edge of her chair. She felt that something big might be ready to break.

"That awful thing she did."

"She did an awful thing?"

"I'll say!" Mildred said. On second thought, she squeezed her lips to a thin line.

"What awful thing did she do?" Anego was determined to get to the bottom of the mystery.

"I don't think I ought to tell."

"It's that awful?"

"I'll say!"

By now Anego was squirming with curiosity. She tried to imagine every awful thing she knew. She could not think of many. At least, not things a teacher might do. She continued to prod. "I won't tell anyone."

"You might."

Anego crossed her heart.

"My mother and father would kill me. They don't know I heard."

"It really must be awful," Anego breathed.

"It is," Mildred agreed, looking very wise.

"Maybe I could guess."

"You never could. It's that awful."

"What's it about?"

"If I tell you that, you might guess."

"Just give me a hint."

"Well . . ."

"Go ahead. I crossed my heart."

The light in Mildred's eyes was encouraging. Anego held her breath, waiting.

"It's about a baby," Mildred said. She glanced quickly toward the kitchen, where Mama was busy trimming the wicks on the kerosene lamps.

Anego was puzzled and a little disappointed. "Does she have a baby?" she asked. "You didn't say she was married."

38

Mildred's pale eyes gleamed. "She isn't," she said. She settled back in her chair and crossed her ankles.

There was a pause while Anego thought about what Mildred had just said. "Then how could she have a baby?" she asked.

"Easy. You don't know very much, do you?" said Mildred with a knowing smile. "But even that isn't the worst part."

Anego swallowed, deciding to say nothing.

"She left it on a doorstep!" Mildred glowed.

"On a doorstep!" Anego was astonished. Leaving a baby on a doorstep like a May basket was something past imagining. "Whose doorstep?" she wanted to know.

But Mildred's lips were sealed. "I can't tell you any more," she said firmly. "My mother and father would kill me."

She began picking the caraway seeds from her cake with a fork. She piled them in a neat pile on the side of her plate.

Anego, deep in thought, watched without seeing. "Did she ever come and take it back?" she asked at last.

"Of course not!" Mildred declared. "She didn't want it. She gave it away for keeps."

"How do you know she meant it for keeps?"

39

"Well, if you leave your baby someplace and then go off without it, that means you don't want it and aren't ever coming back for it, doesn't it? Of course, it was for keeps!" Mildred seemed very sure.

Unexpectedly, Anego felt something warm as the sun light up inside of her. It spread, inch by inch, clear to the tips of her fingers and toes. She loved Mildred. She could hardly wait. She had a million things to show her.

CHAPTER FOUR

The New Car

ﬦ ﬦ   August was a ripening time. Fat, deep red raspberries dropped onto the grass or were snatched and carried off by anxious mother birds. The topmost limbs of the plum trees grew heavy with plums.

Anego climbed the low, spreading branches and shook the ripest plums to the ground, then filled her apron with them. She chose the plumpest and juiciest of the raspberries and lunched in the shade. She lay in the cool grass and watched the clouds changing shape. Magwah and Gyp stirred up bumblebees, or curled by her side.

Pa drove Dick and Daisy back and forth in the hot sun, taking in the harvest and making the hay. First came the mower, flattening the tall grass. Then the rake gathered it up into furrows, ready for Pa to pitch into neat little shocks.

The shocks were loaded into the hayrack and brought back to be stored in the barn loft. That was the part Anego liked best. She sat on the prickly load of hay with the reins in her hand, driving the horses from one shock to the next, while Pa pitched a mountain of hay on the rack.

Anego was very happy. Pa needed her more than he ever had. Anyone could see that. He had no one else to help him, just her. Thoughts of Hamigeesek faded to a comfortable, indistinct blur.

The summer days were long. After supper the sun was still in the sky. Sheila and Anego, in their nightgowns, sat outside on the porch with their hairbrushes. Mama was very strict about keeping their hair clean and shiny. One hundred strokes, no less, was the order of the evening. Mama required, and carefully checked to make sure, that every tangle was brushed out, smooth as silk. Sheila and Anego brushed until their arms ached.

After one busy day Mama went about her usual mending, with the old wicker rocker squeaking as she rocked. She turned to Pa. "It looks to me as though

Anego is the next best thing to a son in the fields these days," she remarked.

Anego paused in the middle of her brushing. The next best thing to a son! She did not even hear Pa's reply. The next best thing! The more she thought about it, the faster she brushed. She almost wished Hamigeesek would come and take her away. Wouldn't they be sorry if Pa had no one to help him at all, not even a girl? But maybe, she thought sadly, her real father would never have given her away in the first place if she had been a son.

Pa was not one to discuss his business very much with anyone, not even Mama. But as the summer passed it became clear to them all that he was, without a doubt, up to something. He made several mysterious telephone calls. Everyone noticed how careful he was to choose times when no one was nearby.

Strange visitors began knocking at the door, asking for Pa. He would whisk them away almost the instant they appeared. Mama, Sheila, and Anego sometimes saw them leaning on the pasture fence in serious discussion.

Afterward Pa was never quite his usual self. He might be quiet and wrapped up in his own deep thoughts. Or he might be more jolly than anyone had come to expect of Pa.

"Never you mind!" he would say, smiling, when questioned. "You will all find out in good time."

Things reached a climax after one of the callers had taken up a particularly long stretch of Pa's time. They clasped hands at the gate in a firm, businesslike grip. Then Pa walked slowly and thoughtfully back up the hill to the house.

Mama met him at the door fairly bursting with curiosity.

Pa smiled slyly. He closed the screen door behind him. He gave it an extra little tug, tightening it against the mosquitoes. He reached into his pocket, drew forth a thick roll of green bills, and tossed it on the table.

Mama gasped. Sheila's and Anego's eyes bulged with astonishment. Surely no one had ever seen so much money at any one time before!

Mama was first to find her voice. "Joseph," she said a little uneasily. "Where on earth did you get all that money?"

"I struck oil," Pa replied.

Mama searched his face with her eyes. One never could quite tell whether Pa was joking or not. Besides,

44

Mama still knew very little about this strange new land. There *might* be oil, for all she knew. "Did you, Joseph?" she demanded sternly. "Did you really strike oil?"

Sheila and Anego, catching the twinkle in Pa's eye, shared his joke. Even Mama herself smiled.

"No," Pa said. "Nothing like that. I only sold the back forty acres."

It took a moment for everyone to realize what Pa meant—that he had parted with a piece of his precious land!

He began to look uncomfortable. He cleared his throat. "Well," he began, "I've been thinking for some time of getting one of those new automobiles. That way Mama can get out to see more people."

A car! Sheila and Anego hardly noticed that Mama was standing perfectly still and speechless, or that tears were streaming down her cheeks. Almost no one they knew had a car. The few times one had found its way into their remote little community, everyone had raced outside to stare. What kind of a strange, noisy machine could that be, speeding along, drawn by some unseen miracle? Sheila and Anego, but most of all Mama, had never even dreamed of having one of their own.

45

It was decided that Pa's brother, Theodore—who lived near Minneapolis, where everyone knew about such things—should buy the car. Uncle Theodore agreed in a prompt reply to Pa's letter. Even more, he would drive the three hundred miles himself to deliver it, and stay as long as was needed to teach Pa to drive.

The days dragged endlessly while Uncle Theodore, who was just as slow as Pa, took his time about choosing one that was exactly right.

At last his letter came, bearing the happy news that their car—and a fine one it was—had been selected and would be ready for the long trip within days.

Mama's eyes shone with a new light. She sang her Irish songs as she went about her chores. She laughed a great deal more than usual. She played her harp from the wicker rocker on the porch each evening. Sheila and Anego kept time with their hairbrushes, and hummed along. Pa, explaining that his voice was a lot like a crow's, did not join in. But he seemed to enjoy the concert as much as anyone.

Eventually the day dawned when the car and Uncle Theodore were due to arrive. Sheila and Anego were outside very early, swinging on the gate at the end of the driveway.

They heard it long before it appeared. The strange

roar of an engine brought a hush over everything else. Even the birds were still and listening. It seemed to Sheila and Anego that everyone for miles around must know that the Veselkas' new car was about to appear.

The narrow road had been made for buggy wheels. Uncle Theodore, to be on the safe side, sounded his horn before rounding each corner. It was the thrilling *beep-beep* of the horn that came first. Then the car itself swung into view, almost lost in a cloud of dust. It was the grandest sight that Sheila and Anego had ever seen, or even imagined.

Uncle Theodore, looking grim and dusty, gripped the steering wheel. He guided the strange black machine through the gate and up the driveway toward the house.

Sheila and Anego tore off to meet him. Uncle Theodore stopped the car obligingly and invited them to stand on the running boards for the rest of the way. Nearly bursting with pride and delight, they rode up the hill, hanging on for dear life.

They tried to notice everything. The seats were covered with black leather. There were two small round isinglass windows in the back. As they were to learn later, there were even curtains with windows in them, neatly rolled, to be fastened to the sides in case of

47

rain. No question about it, someone had thought of everything.

Pa and Mama were waiting at the top of the hill.

"It goes so fast," Mama worried aloud. "Suppose it should run into something!"

Uncle Theodore stepped out and shook hands all around. He smiled, wiping the dust from his glasses. "Joseph always liked a fast horse, Katherine," he said. "This machine will be no different once he gets it broken in."

But learning to drive was not as easy as Pa had imagined, or as Uncle Theodore had made it seem. Pa was used to feeling the tug of the reins. He was skilled in winning the confidence of an animal that was pleased to obey his will. Dick and Daisy knew the way to most places. Much of the time there was no driving to do at all.

Pa found the steering wheel strange and mindless. He sat upright and stiff. He felt a frightening responsibility.

It was a long time before Mama felt safe in letting Sheila and Anego ride along. "I'm not dressed," she said, turning down her own invitation. "Everyone would see me!"

By this time Sheila and Anego did not feel too sure

themselves. They climbed into the back as stiff and up-right as Pa. They gripped the edge of the seat with both hands and said nothing. But they were ready and determined to experience whatever might be in store for them.

All went well enough at first. Uncle Theodore sat beside Pa, keeping a sharp eye on his handling of the controls. Sheila and Anego relaxed. The speed was a new sensation they began to enjoy almost at once. When they passed a buggy Sheila waved joyfully. Almost everyone was too busy staring to wave back.

It was around a sharp curve that Pa forgot which pedal was the brake. He took his eyes from the road for just one moment to look.

"Watch out!" Uncle Theodore shouted, grabbing the wheel.

But it was too late. The car swerved and left the road, jogging helplessly to a halt in a shallow ditch, half-filled with water from the last rain.

Pa looked back over his shoulder immediately. "Are you hurt, children?" he asked in a tight voice.

Sheila and Anego had hardly felt the bump. They shook their heads, feeling very sorry for Pa.

Uncle Theodore drove while Pa, Sheila, and Anego pushed. They laid branches in front of the back wheels to help them grip. The car rocked forward and back-ward, backward and forward. It took some time before it was back on the road and ready to be off again.

"You drive," Pa said to Uncle Theodore.

Uncle Theodore was indignant. "When you are thrown from a horse, it is very important you get right back on at once," he said.

So Pa reluctantly took the driver's seat again and started off very slowly.

Uncle Theodore turned in his seat. "Not a word of this to your ma," he warned. "Is that perfectly clear?"

Sheila and Anego replied with quick nods.

Summer was fast drawing to a close. A new pace and purpose began to make themselves felt. Like wind pick-

ing up before a storm, autumn gathered speed, sweeping everything toward a cold-weather point of view.

School was just around the corner. Already the fat new mail-order catalogs had arrived, hinting that time was marching ahead. Winter, with all its bluster, was on its way.

Sheila, somewhat uneasily, began to think of the year ahead. She would be an eighth-grader, just one step below the teacher herself. Thrilling, and a little terrifying, was the thought that this would be her last year at the familiar little schoolhouse. She hardly dared think beyond that. Mama often hinted at the strange new adventures that were fast approaching.

Sheila pored over the latest copies of Mama's magazines, looking for clues to what the outside world was

doing. She noted what they were wearing while they were doing it. She spent hours before the mirror, practicing the look and trying out the hairstyles.

Helen Lindquist was Sheila's classmate. Since there was no one else near her own age within easy reach, she was also her best friend. Helen had been born lucky. Not only did she have an aunt who lived in Minneapolis, but she received occasional invitations to visit as well. Each time Helen returned she was a ready source of fascinating information about what was new in the city.

"She is my cousin," Mildred often reminded Anego. Which, indeed, no one could deny. Unfortunately, however, the branch of the family tree that Mildred shared with Helen was bare of city aunts.

Sheila, going through the catalogs, needed to keep Helen in mind. There were some things like long underwear that Sheila knew it would be hopeless to resist. But wherever a small gain seemed possible, she was prepared to try.

"Do I have to wear boots this year, Mama?" she asked. "Helen wore low shoes all last winter."

Just as she had feared, Mama was firm.

"It's Helen's mother's business," she replied stiffly, "if she wants Helen home all winter with pneumonia.

It's utter nonsense going out half-dressed in freezing, bitter weather."

Sheila sighed. It had not seemed to her that Helen was suffering in any way that anyone could notice, from pneumonia or anything else. But she said nothing. She simply chose the boots with the lowest tops of any in the Sears Roebuck catalog.

This year one thought comforted her, making everything else more bearable. She, Sheila Veselka, would be the one to ride to school that first day, seated beside Pa on the black leather seat of their new car. No one, not even Helen Lindquist, could equal that.

CHAPTER FIVE

Adventures of Autumn

🪶 🪶 Anego was up long before she needed to be on the first day of school. She followed Pa forlornly as he went about his early-morning chores. She kept Gyp and Magwah close by her side every minute.

"You won't be gone forever, you know," Pa reminded her with a smile.

Anego's feelings about the opening of school were mixed. Being confined inside on a pleasant day was almost too painful to think about. Just the same, she could not help being caught up in some of the excitement. It had seemed to crackle through the air for days, like lightning before a thunderstorm.

Her clothes, barely unpacked from the big Sears Roebuck boxes, looked and smelled very new. Her pencil box was filled with whole crayons and pencils. The pencils were so new they had never even been sharpened.

Then, impossible to forget, there was the chilling thought of herself and Sheila riding to school in Pa's new car. Anego did not like people who showed off. She was bothered by the uneasy feeling that riding to school in the car might be showing off in the worst way.

Sheila had no such thoughts, and climbed into the front seat beside Pa with the air of a movie star. Showing off or not, Sheila felt this morning was sure to be a memorable one, and she intended to enjoy it to the fullest.

Mama saw them off proudly, waving until they had turned the first bend in the road. Anego, with the back seat all to herself, waved to Mama through one of the round isinglass windows.

It turned out to be even worse than Anego had feared. Everyone was standing on the schoolhouse steps to watch. All eyes were on them as Pa braked to a careful stop.

Sheila climbed down first. Even though she noticed, at a glance, that Helen's shoes were low and her socks knee-high, this time it did not matter. Helen was looking just as impressed as everyone else.

Anego slid from the black leather seat and out the door, facing the curious eyes. She turned to wave timidly to Pa as he wheeled grandly out of the schoolyard. It was not like Pa to be showing off. His satisfied smile made her uncomfortable.

She hurried to find Mildred before the bell rang.

"I sure wouldn't want to ride around in some old thing that makes all that dust," Mildred said, wiping her eyes and coughing.

The car was not what Anego wanted to talk about, and so she overlooked Mildred's remark. "The teacher is not fat," she said accusingly.

"Whoever said she was?" replied Mildred, looking surprised.

Anego swallowed hard, but said nothing. It was not worth an argument. I bet Mildred made the whole thing up, she thought, even the part about the baby.

No one was in the mood for games at recess. There was just too much catching up to do. Sheila and Helen, being eighth-graders, chose the spot, a sunny corner of the schoolhouse where they could lean comfortably. The smaller girls followed and gathered around them in an admiring circle.

No one could help noticing that Helen's blond hair was waved flat to her head in smooth, regular waves.

"My aunt gave me a finger wave," she explained before anyone had time to ask. "It's the very newest thing. Marcelling is out. No one wears her hair that way anymore." For one brief moment her eyes rested on Sheila's carefully marcelled hair. "Everyone in Minneapolis is doing a new dance called the Charleston," she hurried on to report.

"Show us! Show us!" the lower-grade girls squealed, hopping up and down. "Show us how to do it!"

"I'm really not very good," Helen replied modestly. But she danced the steps with zest and vigor. Hands forward, she twisted on her toes in the new low shoes. She flung her legs nimbly to all sides, bending from the knee. "Ish-ca-bibble!" she gasped breathlessly at the end. "I do it terrible!"

But everyone, even Sheila, was properly impressed. No one knew, except Helen herself, that the best was yet to come.

She saved it until the last recess. She gathered everyone close, warning the smaller girls on the outside of the staring circle to be on the lookout for boys. Then, with a daring anyone could admire, she lifted her skirt for all to see.

No one could quite believe what they saw. The only underwear anyone had seen so far was bloomers.

Bloomers were loose and roomy, clasping just below the knee with a band of elastic. Sometimes they matched the dress. Mostly they were of sturdy material, and they were usually warm.

In astonishment the girls stared at Helen's long, bare legs, topped only by a brief pink and lacy something-or-other.

"They are called panties," Helen informed them. "Everyone in Minneapolis is wearing them."

Much later, when the Veselkas had finished their supper, and all Mama's questions about the new grades and the new teacher had been answered, Anego followed Sheila outside for a last look around before dark.

Anego could not help noticing that Sheila was being very mysterious about something, acting as though she knew something Anego did not.

"Did you see what Helen was wearing today?" Sheila finally asked, softly. She glanced back quickly toward the sound of Mama's voice.

Anego nodded, saying nothing.

"Well," Sheila said, "I have panties too!" With one quick sweep of her skirt, Sheila flashed her secret.

Anego gasped. Sheila had rolled the legs of her warm bloomers up to their very limit. Sheila's legs looked almost as long and bare as Helen's.

"I'm going to tell Mama!" Anego declared, trembling with shock and horror.

"Go ahead," Sheila replied, dropping her skirt. "See if I care!"

But Anego did not tell. She wondered how it would feel to have bare legs with only a skirt on top. Then, just before she went to bed, she locked her door and rolled her own bloomers just as high as they would go. It felt strange and cool. She thought of what Mama would say if she knew. She rolled them back down in a hurry, feeling ashamed.

She got ready for bed, thinking about Sheila. Sheila did a lot of daring things that Mama never knew. Knowing them made Anego feel almost as responsible for Sheila as Mama did.

By the coming of fall, the wild rice had ripened. The shallow river waters were choked with thick green stalks. Wild ducks gathered in restless flocks. This was their time to feast and fatten before their long flight to the warm south.

This, too, was the time when bands of Indians gathered from everywhere. They pitched their makeshift tents on the banks of the river. They paddled out each day in small boats to harvest the rice.

This year Anego watched them come with fear in

her heart. Would Hamigeesek be among them? Could it be his plan to take her away with him when the rice had been picked?

Sometimes she dreamed of being paddled off down the river in the boat of one of the Indians. She would see Mama, Pa, and Sheila waving from the shore. Then they would fade away, never to be seen again. She would wake in the middle of the night, feeling terrified. She would pull the quilt over her head and curl into a ball, shivering at the lonely yelp of a coyote or the sad hoot of an owl.

But Pa said nothing about Hamigeesek. So Anego, too, said nothing. She went out with Pa and Sheila in their boat just as she always had. They bent the rice stalks, heavy with ripe grain, and beat them with flails until the rice dropped into the bottom of the boat. They took their small harvest to the rice mill down the river. There they waited their turn to have it roasted to a crunchy, golden brown.

The Indians watched Anego curiously. She could hear them questioning Pa. She could hear Pa explaining slowly and carefully, in Chippewa words, and they seemed to be satisfied.

Fearful, yet fascinated, she watched the Indians from the safety of Pa's boat. She watched the many small, barefoot brown children, who hardly dared raise their shy, dark eyes to a stranger.

"Why don't they go to school?" Anego asked Pa.

"Some do," Pa replied. "There are schools, now, starting up on the reservations. Mostly they learn everything they need to know from their parents and the tribe. But things are going to be different for them in the future. The white man has taken most of their land. They cannot just hunt and fish and gather the wild rice as they always have before. They are going to have to learn new ways in order to survive."

"You are a white man, aren't you, Pa?"

"It doesn't matter," Pa said. "This earth belongs to everyone. No one has a greater claim to it than any other. We must never forget that."

As soon as the wild rice was harvested, the Indians moved on. Anego breathed a secret sigh of relief. Ha-migeesek had not been among them. Maybe he had changed his mind or forgotten.

With the coming of the first frost, the homesteaders, like prudent squirrels, got down to the serious business of winter. Houses and barns were sealed tight as drums against the cold blasts of biting winds to come. Enough wood for months of warm fires was chopped to the proper size and piled neatly in woodsheds close to the houses. Everything was done with the drifting snows and blinding blizzards in mind.

Deer-hunting season fell at about the same time as the first snowfall. The quiet little community was suddenly invaded by a crowd of strangers from the city. Loud, laughing men with red caps and bright jackets threw bottles and terrified the homesteaders with their careless smoking and matches.

Anego saw beautiful deer with terror in their eyes, fleeing for their lives, lost and confused. She saw them limp and lifeless, tied to the tops of cars loaded with noisy hunters on the inside.

"Murderers!" Mama complained bitterly.

"Buck fever," Pa said. "That's what those city fellers have. When they have guns in their hands, they will shoot anything."

The cows and horses and Magwah were kept in the barnyard. Gyp was tied. The gates to the barnyard were closed.

"We can't tie Magwah," Pa said. "The gates and fences won't hold him if he chooses to go. We will just have to hope the bell will be enough."

So, one morning, it was no real surprise for anyone to discover that Magwah was missing. When Anego called, he did not come bounding joyfully to meet her.

"He may still be back," said Pa with forced cheerfulness. "No one knows his way around the woods better than Magwah."

Throughout the day at school, Anego felt fear rising, like a determined bubble, to the top of her mind. She remembered all that Pa had said about the dangers of the woods at that time of the year. Magwah had always come before when she called. She was certain, with a deep, heavy dread, that he would not stay away so long without a very good reason.

He was still missing at the end of the school day. Even Pa seemed worried. He agreed it was time to have a careful look through some of the woods nearby. It was the supper hour, and there would be no hunters out before dark.

The wind had died, and the woods had quieted to an expectant hush. A sharp crispness in the still air meant the temperature was on its way down. "Perhaps, even snow," Pa said, peering at the milk-white sky.

The hunters would be pleased about that, Anego knew. They always hoped for a thin layer of snow to make tracking the deer to their hiding places easy. Anego hoped with all her heart it would not snow.

She stayed very close beside Pa. They looked everywhere, calling Magwah's name. They stopped to listen often. They heard nothing but the sleepy caw of a late crow or the early hoot of an owl.

"It's no use," Pa said at last. "If he had been anywhere nearby, he would have come when we called."

Anego nodded unhappily. Gray dusk was already blotting out some of the details. It would soon be dark, and there would be hunters. There might even be coyotes and wolves.

Then Pa stopped, motioning her to be quiet. He parted the bushes with a sweep of his arms. He turned to Anego with sadness in his eyes. "It's him," he said quietly.

Magwah was lying sprawled in a pitiful heap. There was no joyful leaping about at the sight of his friends. There was not even the welcoming lift of his head. Only his eyes moved at all. Eyes that had been alert and lively were now dull and glazed with pain.

While Anego gently raised his head to rest in her lap, Pa bent to examine the wound on the animal's limp body.

If anyone could do anything, Anego thought desperately, Pa could. People for miles around always brought their sick and wounded animals to him because he was better than anyone at making them well.

"He is in pain, Anego," Pa finally said. "He won't get better."

Hot tears overflowed Anego's eyes and burned down her cheeks. She bit her lip to keep from crying out loud. I must be brave, she told herself. She knew what Pa was thinking he must do. He knew what was best. She could depend on him.

Pa took her hand in his, and they went back to the house together.

In her room, with the door closed and bolted, Anego lay across the bed. She buried her head in the pillow and pressed her hands tightly over both ears.

She dimly heard Pa leave the house, closing the door softly behind him. It seemed forever before she heard the sound she had known would come, a single sharp crack of Pa's rifle . . . then silence, a dreadful, empty silence.

CHAPTER SIX

Christmas Secrets

➷ ➷   Almost as though it had never happened before, excitement gripped the small community with
the first snowfall. Great fluffy flakes, big as popcorn,
floated down over the countryside. Everything, from
fence posts to rooftops, was frosted a matching marsh-
mallow white.

Caps were pulled low and scarves wound high, cov-
ering ears and noses from the sharp wind. Wet mittens
were strung up on a line behind the range, and wet
overshoes cluttered the kitchen.

As soon as it was clear that winter had settled
in, all thoughts turned expectantly toward Christmas.
It was a holiday that shone as brightly as the star
of Bethlehem at the very peak of the long gray winter.

Sheila and Anego checked the days off the calendar, one by one.

"Twenty-seven days," Anego said with a sigh. It seemed half a lifetime, at the very least.

"One!" Sheila reported a long, long time later. Only one more day to wait!

The Christmas program was the high point of all school activities. This year, as every other, the school-house had buzzed for weeks with joyous plans, as decorations were made and would-be performers were coached to perfection.

The Veselkas' car had been carefully stored away until the return of warm weather and passable roads. So Dick and Daisy were harnessed, once again, to the little cutter. Pa hung bells on the harness for a festive air. The sled skimmed lightly over the snow on its way to the schoolhouse, the bells jingling merrily.

There was a silver moon shining over the treetops. It lit the evening sky, making it nearly as bright as day. The new snow sparkled like the tinsel on Sheila's and Anego's angel costumes, tucked beneath the seat at Mama's feet.

Sheila and Anego rode curled in the hay in back, under one of Grandma Veselka's featherbeds. Mama and Pa were wrapped in cocoons of heavy woolen blankets. They rode perched on the seat in front.

The schoolhouse was a magnificent sight to behold. It was lit from top to bottom with gasoline lanterns. The light beamed from the windows, reflecting on the snow.

The Christmas tree reached to the ceiling. It glittered and twinkled with tinsel and candles. Heaped at its foot were presents wrapped in fancy paper and tied with colored ribbons.

There was not a solemn face anywhere. Eyes shone as brightly as the star perched on the lopsided top of the tree. Good will, laughter, and joy rollicked from every corner of the small schoolhouse.

Santa, with a not-very-real cotton beard, passed out the presents. Anego could see in an instant that he was Mildred's father. Her present was a box of dominoes and a bag of popcorn.

On the way home Mama, in her clear voice with its Irish lilt, sang "Silent Night." Sheila and Anego joined in. A warm light shone in Pa's eyes. He held the reins loosely while Dick and Daisy cantered along at their own sprightly pace.

Not until after Sheila and Anego had gone to bed would the packages that had been collecting at the Veselkas' for so long be brought out, unwrapped, and stuffed into the stockings. The very thought of the decorated tree and bulging stockings, on any day of the year, was enough to send chills quivering up Sheila's and Anego's spines.

Very early on Christmas Eve, after the stockings had been hung, they hurried off to bed in their long flannel nightgowns.

Mama called a stern warning after them. "Mind now, no getting up in the middle of the night, do you hear? See that you wait until Pa has a nice warm fire going. There's no sense in catching your deaths of cold!"

Sheila and Anego had shared a special secret since the year it had become clear to them both that Santa was, in fact, just Mama and Pa. They lay flat on their stomachs and pressed their ears firmly to a small opening between the warm brick chimney and the boards of the floor. There they waited breathlessly to hear snatches of what Mama and Pa were saying below.

"Anego will love this," Mama said above an exciting crackle of paper. "Did you notice that it opens? Will you just look at what is inside!"

Anego shivered from head to toe.

And then again, "Do you think this is too grown-up for Sheila?" Mama asked.

Sheila held her breath, waiting for the next clue.

"No, I think not," Mama continued. "We might as well let her have it. Helen Lindquist is getting one too, her mother told me."

It was easy enough to tell when the stockings had been filled and the tree decorating begun. "Here is the star," Mama's voice was saying. "Why don't we put it on first?"

Then Pa's voice reached them, stern and loud for Pa. "Katherine! Get down from that ladder! You know how careful you should be in your condition!"

Mama's voice came through, soft and clear, a few seconds later. "Just think, Joseph, next year there will be three stockings instead of two!"

In the dim moonlit hallway Sheila and Anego lifted their heads and exchanged puzzled glances.

"Do you think it will be a son?" Mama's voice went on.

"Maybe," Pa replied, "though I wouldn't count on it too much. A girl will be just fine with me."

For the first time Sheila and Anego did not wait until the very end. Without a word they tiptoed back across the cold floor to their own rooms.

Mama was going to have a baby! It was an overwhelming thought. Mildred's mother had them frequently, but not Mama. They had never thought of Mama having one. They felt confused, lonely, and left out of the big plans that were being made without them. Until then they had felt important parts of the family. Suddenly they were on the outside, on the edge of things. Even the thought of their stuffed stockings and the gaily decorated Christmas tree was not enough to erase the uncertainty they had begun to feel.

On Christmas morning the big old heater glowed red with the fire Pa had gotten up before dawn to build. Tinsel shimmered from every twig of the big tree. The candles had been lit. The glass balls and birds with spun-glass tails were just as breathtaking as always. But Sheila and Anego sat quietly in the middle of mountains of fancy wrappings, ribbons, and unwrapped presents, and felt like crying.

Mama's eyes were as bright as the candles on the tree. For weeks she had spent all her time planning for this day. She had made careful selections from the mail-order catalogs. Packages had piled closer and closer to the ceiling of her closet. For months she had spent all her spare time making fancy aprons with pockets in the shape of squirrels, elephants, or flowers. She had made handkerchiefs with daintily crocheted edges. She had made pincushions in a splendid variety of shapes and colors.

But if Sheila and Anego had not had their minds on other things, they might have noticed that, in spite of

Mama's bubbling joy, there was just a trace of uneasiness at the bottom of it. It would have been even more noticeable, had they been in the mood to notice, when Mama left the room to make one more quick trip back to her closet.

"We have saved the very best until last," she announced when she reappeared.

She laid a package on Anego's lap. It was a plain package wrapped in ordinary brown paper. It was tied with brown twine.

"It came for you, Anego," Mama said gently, her joy simmering down to a shaky smile. "It is from Hamigeesek. Now, what do you think about that?"

Anego shrank back as though she had been struck. She stared fearfully at the package perched on her knees. Hamigeesek had never sent her anything before. Always he had been far off in time, too far to touch her life in a real way. Now he seemed to be reaching out into the heart of her safe and familiar world. The package was real. There was no doubt about that.

There was not a sound. The room seemed to be holding its breath, jut as were the people in it. Anego's trembling fingers fumbled with the knots in the twine. She could feel the warm and loving circle of watching eyes. She shivered, feeling cold in spite of the warmth coming from the red-hot heater. Slowly she unwrapped the brown paper and lifted the cover of the box.

"Moccasins!" Mama breathed softly. "Isn't that lovely! Real Indian moccasins!"

Anego's eyes fastened on the moccasin in her hand. It was made of soft leather. It was trimmed with yellow, red, blue, and green beads. It was just the right size for her foot.

Sheila reached into the box. "Look, there's a note!" she said, holding up a small piece of folded paper.

"A note? You never told me Hamigeesek could write," Mama said, glancing quickly at Pa.

"It would have been easy enough for him to find someone to write it for him," Pa said.

"Of course." Mama nodded. "Read it, Sheila."

"Anego," Sheila read. "You have been very brave. Words cannot say what is in my heart. I will see you when the crows return. I have news of great joy."

The room was hushed. It seemed to Anego her heart must be hammering as loudly as a drum for everyone to hear.

"Well, he doesn't say he is going to take Anego away with him," Sheila said. "He only says that he will see her when the crows return. Maybe he's only coming to visit."

No one said very much more. At least they all knew

it would be a long time before the crows returned.

Later that day, while Mama and Sheila were fixing the chicken for stuffing, Anego slipped quietly upstairs and into Mama's room. She stood in front of the mirror and studied the face that was reflected back at her. It was very brown. Sheila's face had turned from summer brown to white long ago. But Anego could see that hers was a deep, rich, even color. She could see that her eyes were not blue. They looked as deep and dark as the bottom of Pa's well. She reached up to touch her hair. It was smooth, and coarse, and straight. It was as black as a crow's wing.

Suddenly, as though she had never known it before, the thought burst into reality. I am not white like Mama and Pa and Sheila. I am an Indian!

A strange new sensation shivered through every part of her, clear to the tips of her moccasined toes.

CHAPTER SEVEN

The Doctor Comes

As winter gripped the countryside, it seemed to everyone, but most of all to Mama, that green grass and flowers had left the earth forever.

Snow, driven by the wind, swept from the frowning gray clouds and erased low places from the landscape. Drifts piled high over the fence posts.

Pa leaned into the stinging winds, making his daily rounds from house to barn, from barn to house. The temperature dropped to thirty, forty, fifty below zero. "They say we are having the coldest weather in twenty years," he boasted, as though he'd had a hand in its making.

Mama kneaded soft white dough for bread, warm and floury, on the kitchen table. She filled the lamps with kerosene and trimmed their wicks with a sharp scissors.

Sheila and Anego watched without seeming to. Mama was growing fat and heavy. She moved slowly and rested often. Even if they had wanted to, they could never have imagined Mama's baby. Not even when she called them together and told them herself, expecting them to be surprised and pleased.

"You are almost grown up," she said to Sheila. "Think of how a little baby will look up to you. Think how it will depend on you."

But Sheila made no reply.

"It will be just like a big doll!" Mama said, turning to Anego. "Why, it might even be a brother!"

Anego, too, said nothing.

As it always had before, the sun's warm rays finally slipped through; the snow on the rooftops melted at noon and than dripped into icicles in the evening.

The heavy snow settled. Sheila and Anego made snowmen with carrot noses and sticks for eyes. The boys battled at recess in snowball wars. They built solid snow forts and stacked heaps of icy ammunition behind them.

Mama was huge, uncomfortable, and complaining.

Pa was trying his best to be as helpful as he could, and to be cheerful at the same time. "Any day now," he told her, "the roads will be clear and ready for cars. The baby won't be here for weeks. We have plenty of time."

He was not too concerned when Mama announced one morning that she felt "different." She decided it might be better not to get up at all, just in case. Pa agreed and went about his work in the usual way.

Toward noon the sun was blotted out by dark clouds churning up over the horizon. Pa peered anxiously at the sky. He tried to tell himself there could be no more snow in the offing, that it was not the season for another blizzard.

In late afternoon he hitched Dick and Daisy to the cutter and made off toward the school. There was not much doubt in his mind then that snow was on the way. Pa's long experience warned him to prepare for the worst.

By the time they arrived home, small stinging pellets of sleet were beginning to hurl down in sheets. The wind was rising. The sun had disappeared, darkening the early-evening sky long before its time.

Pa lit the lamps and began the supper chores. He tried to comfort Mama, but his words sounded as though he did not believe them himself. The snow would be stopped by morning, he said. It could never amount to much this late in the season.

By bedtime it was clear that a full-blown blizzard was fast rising to its peak. Wind whistled and howled. It rattled and banged loose boards and shingles. Snow whirled down the chimney and beat against the windows.

Pa carried armloads of wood and stacked them behind the kitchen range. He stoked the fire in the living room, setting off a burst of crackling sparks.

"You go along to bed," he told Sheila and Anego. "I'll stand by and keep the fire going tonight."

"All night?" Anego asked. "Are you going to stay up all night?"

"I can sleep," Pa said with a smile. "Dick and Daisy never go to bed, but they sleep, don't they?"

They said good night to Mama.

"Don't you worry, now," Mama told them with a telltale quiver in her voice. "I lived in Cork, you know. That's why I always bob to the top just like one."

She forced a laugh. Sheila and Anego forced smiles in return.

When Anego opened her eyes in the morning, the light was very bright. She looked toward the window. It was covered with thick frost, patterned like ferns. Snow was drifted high on the outside sill. The sun

shining through the window made it look like dia-
monds.

Anego hopped out of bed and hurried over to look.
She blew her warm breath on the window and cleared
a patch with her hand.

There were no clouds in the sky. It was a vast, vivid,
clear blue. Everything was buried in deep, deep snow.
It sparkled in the bright sunlight like acres of
Christmas tinsel.

The living room was warm. Pa turned as Anego entered. His face was grim and tired, and his clothes were
rumpled.

"I called the doctor," Pa said. Anxiously, he looked
out at the deep snow.

Mama refused her breakfast, complaining of pains.

"I called the doctor," Pa told her again and again. "I
called last night. I called again this morning. He said
he would try to get through. He will need a sled and a
couple of very good horses."

Some time later Pa reported his latest news. "The
doctor is on his way. I called again. He started off just
after daybreak. He should be here before dark."

Sheila and Anego did not go to school. They huddled in the kitchen. They went through the motions
of Mama's chores. Pa hurried back and forth to Mama.

He prepared food in as many tempting ways as he could think of, but he brought it all back, mostly untouched.

"The doctor won't be here until late," Pa told them at the end of the afternoon. "He will need a room for the night. You girls move in together. You can leave one of your rooms for him."

Sheila and Anego nodded. Having a doctor in the house for the whole night made his visit seem even more frightening. Anego moved what she would need into Sheila's room. It was comforting to know that Sheila would be nearby.

Pa paced from one window to the other. At last he said, "You two watch for the doctor. I will be with Mama." His blue eyes filled with tears. He turned aside quickly to keep the girls from noticing, and hurried out of the room.

Sheila and Anego, shivering with even greater fear and uncertainty, stared at each other. Pa was crying! Something must be very wrong. Pa, of all people, never cried.

A long time after, when the sun had slipped off over the edge of the white world, streaking behind a trail of rose-pink light, Sheila and Anego watched the doctor arrive. His horses, breathing clouds of steam, struggled uphill through the snow toward the house.

The doctor looked like a huge, gruff bear bundled into a black fur overcoat. He wore a hat with ear flaps, and enormous fur mittens. He stomped the snow from his boots on the front step.

Pa hurried out to take charge of the doctor's horses. The doctor, his face cherry red from the cold, took his mysterious black bag and went straight to Mama's room.

"Sheila and Anego," Pa said when he came back inside, "you two run along and hop into bed."

"But, Pa!" Anego began.

"It isn't anywhere near bedtime!" Sheila protested.

"Never mind," Pa replied. "Do as I say, do you hear?"

Pa almost never spoke harshly to them. When he did, no one argued. Pa had never been known to change his mind once he had made it up.

So Sheila and Anego went quietly off to bed at six o'clock in the evening.

They heard hurrying footsteps and low voices. Once or twice they heard Mama cry out.

Anego moved closer to Sheila. She wondered if Mama might die. She felt cold, frightened, and very lonely. She wanted to ask Sheila if she thought Mama would die, but she could not get herself to say the words.

"Do you think Mama will be all right?" she asked instead.

"Pa was crying," Sheila replied grimly. "I don't think he thought she was all right."

Sheila had voiced Anego's worst fears. She felt helpless and alone. Everything around her seemed to be falling to pieces. Magwah had died . . . and now, maybe it would be Mama.

"If you are going to be a bawl-baby," Sheila snapped, "go and sleep someplace else."

So Anego smothered her sobs and remained silent, asking no more questions.

CHAPTER EIGHT
Mama's Baby

⅍ ⅍ The first faint light of daybreak gleamed a soft silver through the frosted window. The corners of the room were still gray and blurred with shadows.

Anego sat up and rubbed her eyes. Puzzled, she glanced across at Sheila, still asleep by her side, her yellow hair spilling out over the white pillow. Why was she in Sheila's room? In an instant she was wide awake. Mama!

She slid quietly to the cold floor. Teeth chattering, partly from the cold and partly from anxiety, she slipped her feet into the Indian moccasins, hurried into her warm robe, and knotted its sash.

She closed the door gently behind her, being careful not to wake Sheila. Her own door, she noticed at once, was slightly ajar. She tiptoed over to peek inside. There was no one there. The bed had not been slept in. There was no sign of the doctor. Everything was very quiet and peaceful. It was almost as though she had awakened from a bad dream.

Suddenly the door to Mama's room opened. Pa stepped out into the hallway. He paused, startled to see Anego standing in the half-light like a small, lost ghost.

"Anego?" He sounded surprised. His face was lost in the shadows.

"Yes, Pa." Anego's teeth were still chattering.

Pa hesitated for just a moment; then he beckoned her to follow him into Mama's room.

The lamp's wick was turned very low. There was only a little light glowing on the table beside Mama's bed. The lamplight shone on the big old brass bed, reflecting a wavering, golden glow off its shining knobs.

Pa tiptoed ahead to turn up the light. Then Anego could see Mama's face. Her eyes were closed, and her thick, shining hair was wound around her head.

Pa lifted a corner of the quilt for Anego to see.

Anego's eyes widened with astonishment. A tiny red face wrinkled at the light. Two small red fists fluttered

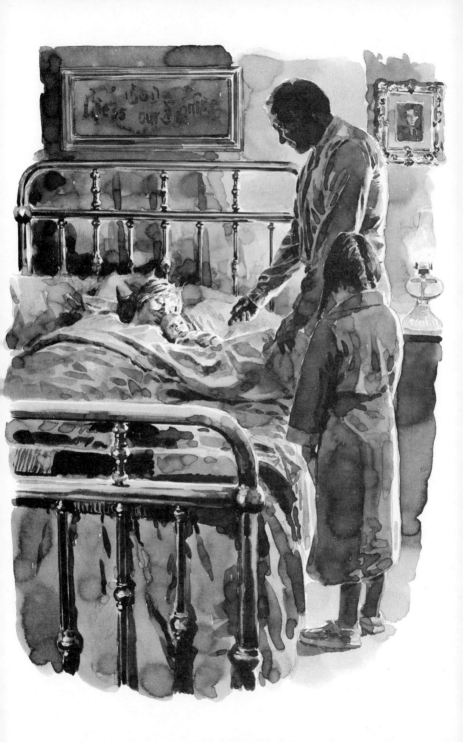

from the blankets. The lamplight shone gold on a wee head covered with tight little curls.

Mama stirred and opened her eyes. "Hello, Anego," she said, smiling. "How do you like your new little brother?"

Anego raised her eyes to Pa's face. But he was not looking at her. He was looking at the baby. His eyes were shining. He was smiling a very proud and happy smile.

Anego was shivering. She felt as cold as ice. Without a word, she turned and ran with all her might down the cold, dark hallway and back into her own room, away from Sheila, away from everyone.

The doctor had left behind some very stern warnings with Pa. Mama must be very careful, he had said. She would need to stay in bed for quite a while.

"I have asked your grandma to come," Pa told Sheila and Anego. "It will be up to the three of you to look after the house until Mama is stronger."

Sheila and Anego had not seen Grandma Veselka very often. She lived three hundred miles away, on the other side of Minneapolis. That was a very long journey for anyone to make, but especially for Grandma, whose time and money were both in short supply. They could not remember much of Grandma. The little they could recall from other brief visits was pleasant. She had laughed a great deal—a jolly, fat kind of laugh. She had coaxed them to eat a lot of unfamiliar foods with strange foreign names. They were cautiously pleased that she was coming back to take charge.

A few days later Pa hitched Dick and Daisy to the cutter for his long drive through the snow to meet the train that would be coming through, bringing Grandma. "Take good care of Mama," he told Sheila. Then he laid his hand on Anego's shoulder and said, "I'm leaving you in special charge of the baby, Anego. I know how much you love baby things."

Anego felt uncomfortable. Pa had always trusted her with baby chickens, young calves, and a lot more. But this time it was different. Mama's baby was wobbly and red-faced. He cried a lot. But, deep down, she knew these were not the real reasons. The minute this baby made a sound, Pa was right there, or Mama. They did not need her. They seemed to have almost forgotten she was there at all. Anyone could see that their new son was the most important person in the world to them.

"We must think of just the right name for him," Mama had said, as she smoothed the baby's gold curls gently with her hand. "I'd say he looks more like a little Mike than anyone." She laughed, and then she paused to study him thoughtfully. "Why, that's exactly right!" she had exclaimed. "Michael Veselka! Who could ask for a better name than that?"

Pa, with stars in his eyes, had agreed that it sounded just fine to him too.

Sheila and Anego were waiting at the window when Pa and Grandma arrived. Grandma, in the front seat beside Pa, was tucked to her chin in warm blankets.

"See how short she is," Sheila said, "and fat!"

"She has a lot of bundles," Anego noted hopefully.

Good cheer followed Grandma into the house like a warm breeze. She hugged Sheila and Anego, feeling as soft as a plump feather pillow. She made clucking and cooing sounds, smiling and tipping her head to one side or the other.

Anego stood stiff as a broomstick with her hands folded behind her back. She watched while Grandma gave orders to Pa or scolded him as though he were a small boy.

Grandma was delighted with little Mike. "He's the exact spittin' image of you when you were that age, Joseph!" she said. She rocked the baby on her broad knees. She held him skillfully and easily, one hand supporting his wobble.

Sheila, glancing at Anego, pressed one hand over her mouth, smothering a giggle. Even Anego smiled. It was hard to imagine Pa's almost-bald head covered with tight gold curls.

Little by little, over the next few days, Grandma unpacked her bags and bundles. Most of what she had brought was food. There were jars of homemade plum jam, sun-dried slices from apples that had been grown on her own trees, and big brown buns filled with a surprise prune filling.

Grandma gave little Mike the best of care. She bathed, dressed, and rocked him, making her little cooing noises all the while.

"Well, Joseph," she said as she tucked the baby lovingly into his crib for one of his many naps, "at last you have a son to carry on the homestead." Her round face, full of pride and satisfaction, beamed at Pa.

Pa watched little Mike trying his best to smile. His two hands fluttered from the blankets like small pink butterflies. "It's a nice dream, Ma," he said, "but Sheila will need a high school next year. I must think of them all."

"You're not considering leaving!" Grandma cried. "Just when the place is beginning to pay off! Think of what all this land will mean to little Mike someday!"

"Things aren't as they used to be, Ma," Pa said. "An

education is becoming very important. I want all my children to have the best of everything."

"Send Sheila to me!" Grandma replied briskly. "There's a good high school plenty close enough. Besides, I could do with the company."

Mama, who was in no mood to think of moving, thankfully agreed. Pa was pleased and very relieved. Even Sheila felt a secret lift knowing that her strange new world would include comfortable, familiar Grandma Veselka.

Anego tried to imagine what it would be like without Sheila. Mama would be busy with the baby. Even Pa was already looking forward to taking little Mike into the woods with him to hunt and fish, or help out in the fields. It was more clear than ever there was no place left for her. Hamigeesek would be coming soon. What would become of her? It was a thought almost too terrifying to think. Yet she could think of almost nothing else.

Sheila was learning to hold the baby. She helped Grandma give him his bath. She brushed his curls.

Anego silently crept away when everyone gathered around little Mike to admire and exclaim. Sometimes her feelings rose to the surface in a way that frightened her. She spent lonely, unhappy hours in her room. She closed her eyes, trying desperately to bring back the brown bird. But it seemed to have left without a trace.

Mildred's predictions were gloomy. "It will be a lot worse when he gets older," she declared. "He only bawls his head off now. Wait until he gets big enough to break all your things!"

But underneath was the ache that told Anego she had disappointed Pa. She had a way with baby things, he had always said. Yet, with little Mike it was different. She made excuses for not helping with him. She even avoided being around him as much as she could. Sometimes she saw Pa watching her with a questioning, unhappy look. But there was nothing she could do to change the way she felt.

As the weeks went by, everyone could see that Grandma was becoming restless.

"I need to go back to my own place, Joseph," she said more and more frequently. "There are things that have to be done before it is too late in the year."

"Of course," Mama and Pa reluctantly agreed.

But Mama was not anxious to take on the full load of household chores by herself. She thought of the daily wash heaped in the big old washtubs. It was not easy wringing clothes through the creaky old hand wringer. It took time to string them to dry near the warm range. She dreaded the thought of getting along without Grandma's strong and willing hands.

Pa, at the last minute, announced the surprise he had planned for Grandma. He had decided to take out the car and drive her back himself. Most of the snow had melted from the roads, and the mud was drying up fast.

Grandma was startled and not altogether pleased. She would have preferred a horse to one of those noisy new machines any day. But when Pa explained how undependable the trains to that remote part of the country were, she agreed.

Pa worried about leaving Mama in charge by herself.

"You go right along," Mama said, a lot more bravely than she felt. "I'll have Sheila and Anego to help out. One of the neighbors can take care of the outside chores. Besides, it won't be for more than a few days."

With the sun hardly over the horizon the next morning, Pa and Grandma were ready to go. If the machine had a flat tire, Pa reasoned, the extra time would be useful. He knew too, though he did not say, that he was probably a more careful driver than some. Uncle Theodore, for instance, might make it in a lot less time.

Pa looked strange and uncomfortable standing beside the new car in his best suit, his bag gripped tightly in one hand.

Sheila felt very proud. She noticed every little thing. She stored it away in her mind to tell Helen later.

Anego stood with her hands in her apron pockets. She felt shy. Pa looked like a stranger. She could not imagine what it would be like when he was away. He had never gone so far without them before.

Mama had bundled little Mike against the chill of the early-morning air. They all waved from the porch as Pa and Grandma drove off, wishing them luck in loud voices.

There was an uneasy difference about the days with Pa gone. There was a shaky feeling of knowing that he would not be there if something dreadful should happen.

But the chores got done. The days passed. They managed, somehow, to deal with everything as it came up. The last day seemed the longest. But, in its time, that day, too, came to its natural end.

"Tomorrow," they said. "Tomorrow Pa will be home."

The last shade was pulled, and the last light blown out, long before their usual bedtime.

Hours later Anego opened her eyes. She lay, not thinking, somewhere between sleeping and waking.

An owl sounded its low, hollow cry. A lone coyote, far away, marked its place in the night.

She sat up, wide awake and listening. From Mama's room she heard little Mike's cry. It was not his usual cry. It was a strange and frightening sound, followed by a hoarse, muffled gasp.

Almost before Anego was out of bed, Mama's light glowed a golden slit under her door.

"What's the matter, Mama?" Anego's voice was anxious. She watched from the doorway. Mama's long white nightgown was ghostly in the lamplight. She lifted little Mike from his crib. Then she turned. Her face was white with fright. Little Mike's head was bobbing over her shoulder.

"Just listen to him!" Mama said with tears in her voice. "He can't breathe!"

Anego watched with growing horror. Little Mike struggled for each breath. Thrashing his tight fists desperately, he made strange rasping sounds. They rattled from deep inside his tiny chest.

Anego stood, frozen to the spot with fear. If only Pa were here, she thought. He would know what to do. He had cured sick and wounded animals. He would know what to do with little Mike.

"Pa would know what to do!" Mama echoed Anego's thoughts. Tears were brimming in her eyes.

Little Mike drew a harsh breath, followed by a long cry. It ended with a dry wheeze that left him struggling and gasping for air.

"We've got to do something, Mama!" Anego cried. "He has to breathe."

In an instant Mama had brushed the tears from her eyes with the back of her hand. "Steam!" she exclaimed. "Help me, Anego. I must light the fire and start the teakettle!"

She balanced the lamp in one hand and clasped little Mike against her shoulder with the other. She made for the kitchen with Anego close at her heels.

There was no time for talking. As Mama directed, Anego slipped into the old rocker drawn close to the range. Mama laid little Mike gently into her arms.

"I'll be just as quick as I can," she said. "Try to keep him from crying."

Mama piled paper and kindling in the stove. She fanned the small, bright flame with her hand. Anego rocked little Mike, soothing him with soft words, humming little songs.

Mama filled the teakettle, keeping an eye on Anego and little Mike. "He must have gotten a chill," she said in a tight voice. "It could be colic, or even—" she paused, meeting Anego's glance with fright in her eyes—"pneumonia!"

Mama and Anego were both remembering other babies, belonging to neighbors, who had had pneumonia. Most of them had died.

"It's probably no more than a cold," Mama said with firm determination. She reached across to lay her hand on little Mike's small, hot forehead.

Anego watched, feeling numb, thinking she must be asleep in the middle of a nightmare.

"He's hot," Mama said, "but it could be just that he's struggling so."

The teakettle was beginning to sing. Steam rose into the air from its spout. They could feel the warmth of the fire crackling and snapping up the sticks in the grate.

What if something happens to him, Anego thought miserably. Her arms ached from holding him. She patted his back as he fought for air. Pa had always trusted her with baby things. Now this most important baby of all was in trouble. Maybe he would even die. How could they ever tell Pa?

Anego wound the white woolen shawl snugly around little Mike. She held him close. She laid her cheek against his hot little face. She rocked him gently, and talked to him while Mama kept the fire going. Billowy clouds of steam puffed from the teakettle.

Far into the night Mama and Anego worked over

little Mike. They helped him through his coughing spells. They relaxed him between. The room grew warmer, and the air steamier. Anego's back and arms ached, and Mama's hair hung in damp curls over her face.

A faint light glowed on the horizon before little Mike finally closed his eyes. He was weak and tired, but he was breathing almost normally.

"He's better!" Mama whispered softly. "He's going to be all right!"

Anego watched little Mike's face anxiously. His eyelids fluttered. Little ripples of movement quivered through his small body from time to time. His curls were damp and tousled, but his expression was peaceful and his breathing quiet.

"Are you sure, Mama?" she asked.

Mama smiled. "I'm sure," she said. For a moment she rested her hand on Anego's shoulder. "Thank you, Anego," she said. "I could never have done it without you. Just as Pa always says, you have a natural way with baby things."

Anego went back to bed. She tiptoed past Sheila's door. Sheila had slept through everything. Anego smiled. She had never been so tired in her entire life, but she felt a strange new peace glowing deep inside. It made her feel older than anyone, even Mama.

CHAPTER NINE

Presents for Everyone

The new day arrived just as bright and early as any other, taking no account of anyone's loss of sleep. Not a sound was to be heard from little Mike. He slept, curled like a kitten, in his nest of warm blankets.

Anego, from long habit, was still the first one out of bed. She had dressed, eaten her oatmeal, and was waiting for her ride to school long before Sheila, late as usual, made her appearance.

"Why do you have to wait until the very last minute for everything?" Mama said with a sigh. "Your getting up just a few minutes earlier would make life so much easier for everyone."

"I always get there the same time as Anego, don't

I?" Sheila replied, stabbing her mound of oatmeal with the spoon and making a face.

Mama said nothing, picturing to herself a very long day ahead. And when the neighbor who was driving the girls to school in Pa's absence stopped his horses at the Veselka gate, it was Sheila who climbed in first, settling herself comfortably in the best seat up front.

To Anego the day stretched endlessly before her. She hid her yawns behind her propped-up geography book and tried very hard to listen to all that was being said, but she had trouble keeping her mind on anything except Pa's return.

"Pa is coming home today," she told Mildred at recess.

Mildred was tying her shoelace. "I didn't know he was away," she said.

"You did. I told you a million times."

Mildred straightened and looked Anego in the eye. "Then I forgot," she replied.

Anego turned away. She was too tired and sleepy to play Mildred's kind of game that day.

Sheila was having no better luck in arousing Helen's interest in the Veselkas' news. "You should have seen Pa before he left," Anego heard her say. "He looks so important when he is wearing a suit."

Helen shrugged, obviously not very impressed at the

thought of Pa's suit. However, she seldom let an opportunity pass for a discussion of her favorite subject. "I have to get some decent clothes before I go away to high school," she said. "I sure don't want to look like a country mouse!" She pointed the toe of her rose-blush-leather strap shoe out front, where she could study it thoughtfully.

Sheila flushed, quietly tucking her shabby boots out of sight. Mama had reminded her that there was still a lot of good wear in them. She had insisted that Sheila finish them out before starting on her new warm-weather lows. Her long underwear, thanks to a break in the weather, had been neatly snipped off at the knee. But Sheila still wore her long brown stockings with a darn in one heel.

"If they think Helen looks like a country mouse," she worried to Anego later, "what will they ever think of me?"

Pa was not there when they arrived home from school.

"He will most likely be late," Mama said. "Chances are, he didn't start back as early as he left. Most people would never get up at the crack of dawn to see him off."

The day wound slowly down to its inevitable end.

Little Mike was more fretful than usual, and so Anego rocked and amused him while Mama went about bringing in the wash, which had been spread out on lines in the sunshine, and preparing the supper.

Now and then she would pause long enough to smile at Anego. "Just wait until I tell Pa what a blessing you have been," she would say. "I'm so thankful! I hope I never have to live through another night like that!"

Anego buried her face in little Mike's blankets, which smelled of soap and fresh air. She was thankful too. Now that little Mike was all right, nothing else seemed to matter very much.

It was not until long after everything had been put in apple-pie order, and little Mike safely tucked off to bed, that they heard the roar of Pa's engine. The car, in low gear, was beginning its long, slow climb up the hill.

They raced outside to watch from the front steps. The car wound its way up the driveway like a dusty, tired traveler. The headlights shone through the darkness like two round owl eyes.

"Stay right where you are," Mama warned. "If you rush out there, you'll only make him nervous, and he might run over one of you."

Pa's best suit was wrinkled and dusty. He looked very glad to be home. "I had a flat tire," he explained with a weary smile. "I should have been home sooner."

Mama could not waste time talking about flat tires. "Little Mike was sick," she announced breathlessly before he had a chance to say more.

The serious tone of Mama's voice was enough to make Pa forget how tired he was. He turned all his attention toward getting the facts.

"He is just fine now, thanks be to God!" Mama hurried on to say, "And thanks to Anego." She put her arm across Anego's shoulders and squeezed softly. "You just don't know, Pa. She was a blessing, pure and simple!"

"Anego helped you with little Mike?"

Mama nodded. "That she did. I just don't know if I could have pulled him through without her."

Pa looked pleased and relieved. He reached out and gave one of Anego's black braids a gentle tug. "I wouldn't have expected anything else from Anego," he said.

After everyone's questions had been answered and gotten out of the way, Pa announced he had presents for them all. It was a surprise no one had expected. Pa was never one to spend his time and money foolishly.

He handed Mama the biggest bag first. "Merry Christmas!" he joked.

Mama unfolded the white cloth inside, shook it out, and held it up. She looked puzzled.

"It's an ironing-board cover," Pa hastened to explain. "It should fit the board a lot better than the old sheet."

"I'm sure," Mama said, folding it back up. "It was awfully nice of you to think of me."

Sheila's was a comb.

"I knew that Sheila likes to fix herself up," Pa said with a sly smile.

Last of all he gave Anego her bag. His face was beaming. He looked very sure of that one. He, if anyone, knew what Anego liked. He stood by, watching her face, waiting expectantly to see how delighted she was sure to be.

It was a rubber doll, a little Dutch-girl doll made of red rubber. Anego turned it over. Just as she had feared, it had a squeak in the back. An ache began to grow, centered in the region of her heart, until it felt almost ready to burst. This was a doll for babies. Pa had brought her a doll that was meant for babies like little Mike!

"I know you like dolls better than anything," Pa said, still beaming. He was certain he had done the nicest thing possible for her. How could he know that no one but babies played with rubber dolls with squeaks?

Anego swallowed. The ache was worse than ever, but she smiled directly into Pa's blue eyes. "I love it," she said. "It's the prettiest doll I ever saw!"

She waited, watching his face. He looked pleased and proud. He had believed her lie. That was the only thing that mattered. She was not so interested in dolls anymore anyway. She had little Mike now, and he was better than any doll. Then, just like magic, she realized the ache had disappeared!

It was not until the next day, after Pa and Mama had talked the matter over alone, that Anego was told about a very important part of Pa's trip.

"I stopped by the Bear Lake Indian Reservation, where I thought Hamigeesek was most likely to be," Pa said. "I was lucky to find him there. We spent a lot of time together and had a nice long talk."

Pa's quiet words sent a thousand prickles shooting through Anego's body. Her startled eyes fixed and froze on Pa's face.

"We did not hear from him for all those years because he felt you would be better off with us while he was going to school. Now he is a teacher at the reservation, and he is ready to share his surprise with you. He would have liked nothing better than to come back with me, but he will have to wait until school is over for the summer."

Pa had disappeared into a blur in front of Anego's tear-filled eyes. She had hardly heard the last of what he said. She only knew that he had gone looking for her father. He must be even more anxious than she had feared for Hamigeesek to take her away.

"You will be very proud of him, Anego," Pa was saying. "He has never forgotten you. Everything he has done for himself has been with you in mind. He knows things are changing fast. He wants only the best for you. I am proud to be his friend. He is one of the finest men I have ever known."

Anego did not wait for more. She turned and ran like the wind, away from Pa, away from everyone. Gyp leaped from his guard position on the front steps and raced at her side, barking joyfully, thinking it all a game.

Anego paid no attention. She ran blindly, not knowing or caring where she was going. Then, when she was too tired to run anymore, she dropped, panting, into the long grass. She buried her face in her arms, and felt her safe, familiar world crumbling to a million pieces.

Tuesday, Star, and Goldie, chewing their cuds nearby, turned their heads and watched with sleepy stares.

CHAPTER TEN

The Brown Bird Sings

🌿 🌿   "Hamigeesek loves you. He is your father. He wants only the best for you. Just remember that," Pa reminded Anego again and again in the days and weeks that followed. "Of course, we want you to stay with us. But more than that, we want whatever is best for you."

"Of course we do," Mama agreed softly, her eyes bright with tears.

Anego glanced forlornly from one familiar face to the other. She searched for some sign that one of them would say, once and for all, "No, you must not go away. We will not let anyone take you from us. You belong here." Only then would everything slip back to normal, with Hamigeesek just a figure in the background as he always had been before.

Anego saw nothing in either of their faces that told her they would offer such easy escape. They were kinder to her than ever, but their efforts were only a painful reminder that the end was near, as soon as the coming of the crows.

Anego watched the weather anxiously. She felt safe only when a late winter storm heaped heavy snow on the buildings, and the wind blew drifts, or early spring rains flooded the countryside, making the roads impassable. But, as she had known they must, the unmistakable signs of spring finally broke through. The last shrinking snowbanks trickled off into pools forming in the hollows. The first arbutus poked its waxy blossoms through bare patches in the snow and filled the woods with its sweet fragrance.

Then, one still morning, she heard the clear sound of a crow's call marking, once and for all, the change of seasons. Anego knew the time had come.

There could be no exact day when they might begin to expect Hamigeesek. The close of his school would be at the time most convenient to the Indians, and not necessarily the same as theirs. There were few trains in that part of the country, and the few there were could not be depended upon. Hamigeesek would most likely travel by foot and canoe, as did most other Indians. No one knew how long it would take.

Meanwhile Anego, just as she always had, helped with the maple syrup. She hung pails below the little upward cuts Pa carved on the trunk of each maple tree. She watched the sap bleed slowly into them. She helped Mama boil it down to a sweet syrup and pour it into jars that would be stored in the cellar. She thought of the tall stacks of steaming pancakes dripping with the syrup that would be breakfast fare for cold mornings of the next winter. Then she remembered, with a dull and hopeless ache, that she would not be there another winter to enjoy them.

The first spring day warm enough for bare feet always was a high point of the season. "They will probably catch their deaths of cold!" Mama worried to Pa, once she had reluctantly given in to the pleadings of Sheila and Anego. Pa watched with a little smile, saying nothing but remembering his own boyhood days. For him, too, running barefoot over the newly thawed ground had been a treat hard to match at any season. This year Sheila and Anego shed their shoes as usual, but something of the joy seemed to be missing.

Later on that first balmy day Pa, in his shirtsleeves,

leaned on his hoe and talked over the rail fence to Mr. Olafson, the neighbor.

Anego climbed on the gate nearby. She curled her bare toes around the smooth rail and swung slowly back and forth. She closed her eyes, listening to the rhythmic sound of the gate's gentle squeaks.

Mr. Olafson not only farmed the homestead next to Pa's, but he owned the general store and post office as well. Mr. Olafson was always well informed and willing to pass on the latest news.

He reached over to give one of Anego's braids a playful tweak as she swung past. "Hear you're about to get some company," he said. "Feller at the store this morning said he bumped into a Chippewa friend of yours down by the old Milltown dam. Seems his canoe was a bit the worse for wear, and he was having to scout around for more birch bark and spruce gum to patch it up. Said he was headed for the Veselkas' and ought to be able to make it through in a day or so."

"That would be Hamigeesek," Pa said, glancing quickly at Anego.

Anego dropped to the ground. She felt cold as a stone, even though the sun was warm. Before another word could be spoken, she had taken off, full speed, toward the house. She forgot to be careful where she was stepping with her bare feet. It did not matter. Nothing mattered anymore now that Hamigeesek was on his way.

Halfway up the hill she stopped. Everything looked exactly the same as it always had. Pa's yellow house, perched high on the hill, looked peaceful. Gyp was curled in a ball, asleep on the front step. Mama was wheeling little Mike up and down the porch in his big black buggy. Pa, at the foot of the hill, was still chatting with Mr. Olafson.

No one seemed to realize, or care, that everything was changing and would never be the same again. Anego felt terrified and helpless. Events were closing in that she could do nothing about. Hamigeesek was coming, and there was no way of turning him back.

Then she remembered Sheila had once said, "Maybe you could hide. We could tell him you had gone away and we don't know where." It was the only answer. It was all that was left for her to do.

She had no idea where she was going, or when she would stop running. She forgot everything except that she must be far away when Hamigeesek came.

At first everything was familiar. There were trails she had walked hundreds of times with Pa. There were the places where she and Sheila had picked arbutus and even a few pink lady slippers. There was the frog pond, and the willow patch where Pa made willow whistles for them every spring.

She reached the fence that marked the end of Pa's land. She hesitated for just a moment, blotting from her mind all Pa's stern warnings. This was different. Unless she went farther than she ever had before, they would surely find her before she was ready to return. So she climbed the fence.

She hurried on. Her feet were bruised and bleeding, but she paid no attention. Her mind was centered on only one thing.

She came upon an old lumber trail winding through the heavy woods. It was overgrown with weeds, scraggly bushes, and thistles. Paying no heed to barbs, scratches, or the hot sting of thistles, she followed it for as far as it went.

When she was too tired to run she walked, stumbling along at a breathless pace with no clear goal in mind. She went a long way, and a long time passed.

Squirrels chattered their indignation. A big black crow cawed from the top of a dead tree. Anego hurried along even faster, remembering that someone might already be coming out into the woods to look for her.

She stopped to catch her breath a few times, but alarming thoughts crowded into her mind, and she could not rest. She pushed on until she was almost too tired to think.

The woods were getting thick and deep. When she caught a glimpse of the sun shining through the trees, she could see it was far lower in the sky than she would have imagined. When it dropped over the horizon, it would be dark. There would be wolves in the woods after dark, and even bears. It was suddenly clear that she could only go deeper into the woods. There was no other place for her to go, unless she retraced her steps and went back to Pa's. She could not stay in the woods forever. She had only a little time left to go back before the woods would be dark.

The terror of the night woods, looming larger and more real than even Hamigeesek, was enough to change her mind and turn her steps toward home. Fearful urgency became uppermost in her mind as she imagined herself alone in the middle of the dark, wild woods. She looked for landmarks to guide her back home, but she could see nothing she remembered having seen before.

It was a long time before she had the courage to admit to herself that she was lost. She began to cry. She cried for a long time. Then, because she was too tired to cry anymore, she stopped.

The woods all looked so much the same. Her

scratches were beginning to sting, and she was hungry. Birds that she had not seen in the underbrush suddenly zoomed into the air from the place where she was about to step.

She kept an anxious eye on the sun. As it sank, her heart sank with it. She heard the slow, low croak of an old bullfrog starting up his evening song. Little animals hurried and scurried, unseen, through the grass and bushes. She thought of Pa. Pa was never afraid in the woods, not even in the dark. If he were not afraid, that must mean there was nothing to be afraid of, she told herself again and again. I must be brave and not afraid. I must be brave. . . .

A sudden sharp whistling snort warned all the deer around that she was coming. She saw a huge buck with wide horns as he sailed into the underbrush and disappeared. Then she heard the thunder of many other running hooves.

Trembling with a new fear, Anego began to run too. She ran without reason, aim, or purpose. Then suddenly she stopped. She rubbed her eyes, not quite believing what she saw.

Someone was coming over the next rise in the trail. She could see it was a man, striding along, slipping in and out of the tangled bushes as quietly and easily as any deer.

It was not Pa. It was not anyone she knew. This man was tall and very straight. He looked proud. His hair hung about his shoulders, straight and black as a crow's wing. He was an Indian.

The man stopped when he saw her. For one breathless moment their eyes met. Then he smiled, his dark eyes crinkling in his face. "I heard you a long way off," he said. "You came like a white person, not like an Indian. You made much noise and broke many sticks."

In spite of herself, Anego smiled. The man's voice had been as soft and kind as Pa's.

"You are lost," the man said without having to ask.

Anego nodded, biting her lip and trying to look brave.

The tall Indian dropped to his knees and searched Anego's face. His eyes looked as deep and dark as the bottom of Pa's well. "Anego?" he asked gently.

Anego nodded again. No one had to tell her. She knew this was Hamigeesek, and she was not at all afraid.

"Why were you running away?"

There was no scolding in his voice. He had known she was running away. It was easy to tell him the truth. "I don't want to go away. I want to stay with Mama and Pa, Sheila, and little Mike."

For a moment Hamigeesek did not speak. Then he

replied, with sadness in his voice, "You do not need to run. I have not come to take you away if you do not want to go. Joseph Veselka and I are brothers. He offered to keep you so you would be safe from the fever that took your mother from this earth. You have learned much from my friend and his family that you will need to know. There have been great changes, and there will be many more. We must plant crops, raise cattle, and learn from books. In the future the graves of our ancestors will be forgotten, and their trails be grown over with weeds."

He is telling me it is all right to stay with Mama and Pa, Anego thought. He is saying that I do not have to go away with him. But she did not feel as happy as she would have expected. His words had left her feeling strangely sad.

"Joseph Veselka and his wife with the sunflower hair have taken good care of you," Hamigeesek said, smiling.

Anego nodded, thinking of Pa. Pa was not tall and mysterious. Pa's eyes were pale, and his hair was thin. It hardly covered the top of his head. He was just . . . Pa. How could anyone explain any of that? So she said nothing.

"Come," Hamigeesek said, getting to his feet. "It is

time I took you home. Darkness will come soon to the woods."

Hamigeesek walked with long, even steps. He made his way through the low-growing bushes and over-hanging branches with quick movements of his tall body. Every motion was soundless and swift. He hardly disturbed a leaf.

Anego had long ago learned to match her pace to Pa's stride, and so she followed close behind.

It was not until they reached a familiar clearing in the woods that Hamigeesek stopped. On all sides were freshly cut, pine-smelling stumps. This was a spot where Pa had spent many busy hours clearing a patch for planting a new crop. The sun, nearing the horizon, had turned red as a poppy, spreading its pink stain across the western sky. Little plants, long hidden in the shade of tall trees, stretched to catch the sun's last rays. The heavy, sweet fragrance of arbutus filled the air.

Hamigeesek folded his strong brown arms across his broad chest and smiled down at Anego. "Listen," was all he said.

Anego listened. She could hear the shrill pitch of countless small insects. She could hear the warbling, chirping, and quiet chatter of birds by the hundreds, mostly hidden from view among the thick leaves and branches overhead.

Hamigeesek unfolded his arms and took a slow step into the clearing. Very softly at first, he began a friendly little chirp. It sounded to Anego exactly like the birds. He reached into his pocket. With a slow, smooth motion he held out a handful of seeds.

The chirps and twitters overhead stopped. In their place was what seemed to be a breathless listening.

Hamigeesek's soft little chirps grew bolder, blossoming suddenly, unexpectedly into a joyful warble.

One by one the birds began to appear. They teetered and rocked on every twig and branch. Their sharp little black eyes searched to locate this strange new bird from the outside. Anego held her breath. Closer and closer the birds hopped from one twig to another. They cocked their small heads and made soft, inquiring chirps.

Hamigeesek's hand was very still. Every muscle in his straight body was frozen to the stillness of a tall forest tree.

Then it happened. One small brown bird dropped from a branch overhead. It perched on Hamigeesek's finger and pecked at the seeds with a quick bobbing motion.

Almost faster than she could think, Anego saw Hamigeesek's hand close gently over the surprised little bird. "Remember?" he asked her, smiling.

Anego held out her hand and took the bird from Hamigeesek. She curled her fingers around it. She felt it, soft and warm, trembling to escape. She felt the quick little heartbeat inside its small feathered breast. She felt Hamigeesek's kind, smiling face looking down at her.

All at once she remembered. She remembered her mother's warm, brown, smiling face. She remembered the music of her mother's Chippewa words, telling her to be brave and not afraid. She remembered the face, every detail. It had been filled with love.

Anego opened her hand. She watched the brown bird shoot into the air like a small, straight arrow. She laughed out loud.

She put her hand in Hamigeesek's, feeling a great pride. She knew that Hamigeesek was her father. She knew that the warm, beautiful memory had been her mother.

They started back toward the finger of smoke from Pa's chimney that was scribbling the sky over the tree-tops.

"It is a good sign," said Hamigeesek, turning to look back over his shoulder. "The brown bird is singing."